THE CASE OF THE FRENCH CONVENT

The Continuing Chronicles of Sherlock Holmes

C. Thorne

To my beautiful new niece. May she still think of me in the twenty-second century....

CONTENTS

THE CASE OF THE FRENCH CONVENT

"There is no predicting the condition of human remains after so significant a time, Watson," my friend Sherlock Holmes said to me, rather unnecessarily, for as a physician I had some knowledge of such matters. "After two-thirds of a century even the most masterful of embalmers might find his diligent handiwork overtaken by the years, and it is likely that little lies in that august tomb save Bonaparte's time-pitted bones, clad in the pretentious blue uniform he favoured."

Holmes had spoken of the late French ruler with a crisp

distaste, as even after so many intervening decades and a warming in relations between France and our own country, his name was anathema to all good Englishmen, for all that the late conqueror had also been a figure of nearly universal fascination in his time and long after.

Our conversation concerning the mortal remains of our nation's one-time enemy took place on the *Pont Neuf* on a July morning, just after dawn, the Seine flowing lazily below us, its waters low with summer, while the grandeur of Paris spread all about us. The topic of time erasing all things had been inspired by a most sensitive case Holmes had been called across the Channel to undertake on behalf of no less than the French government, a task which he performed with characteristic excellence, bringing the delicate matter to a successful conclusion where all save those who had plotted it were concerned.

Reflecting on the fortnight just past inspired me to note:

"It is not every day that even you, Holmes, are tasked with preventing the theft of the body of an emperor from inside his palatial mausoleum."

"Indeed, Watson," he agreed, "the achievement crowned a case singular to my career."

"At least so far," I added musing that one never knew what might turn up next in the dynamic life of Mr. Sherlock Holmes.

The matter had begun some six days before, during a beautiful early July, when Baker Street had been visited by Ambassador Jean-Claude Boucher-Armchambeau, a rather dandified man who represented France at the Court of Saint James, and the more severe Colonel Alain Allard, of the Paris police, a hard-eyed and hook-nosed fellow, who relayed to Holmes that among their criminal informants there had arisen warnings of sinister chatter passing throughout the underworld, concerning an audacious plot primed to be launched, it was said, against the very soul of France itself.

"What is coming threatens to be a crime which would reverberate within every man, woman, and child of the nation," the Ambassador had explained.

"What, is known thus far?" Holmes had asked, fingers steepled and pressed to his broad brow, his concentration upon this news entirely profound.

"The object of this scheming has yet eluded our identification," said Colonel Allard, clearly frustrated to voice so humbling an admission.

"How, then, do you know it is nothing more than a rumour?" I inquired.

Colonel Allard answered:

"I trust, Doctor Watson, in the reliability of those who have tipped us off to the fact that something unprecedented is coming, and so vast shall it be that its prevention has become the focal point of considerable police resources."

"And yet," said the ambassador in summation, "all efforts have failed to penetrate past the chatter and learn what it is to be. Day by day it has become like resting under a guillotine, waiting for the dreadful blade to drop."

"Then I shall journey to France at once!" Holmes had declared, leaping upward and striding toward his bedroom to retrieve a valise he kept there, ever at-the-ready for just such an impromptu departure.

In the company of these Gallic gentlemen, Holmes had left with barely a word to anyone save Mrs. Hudson, who called out wishes for a safe journey, and I departed with him on a diplomatic train arranged to transport us straight to Dover, and then after a swift crossing of the Channel we were soon in Calais, where a second fast-moving train awaited to take us on to Paris. There Holmes was asked to unravel the loose threads of rumour and whispers, and come to the heart of whatever sinister scheme his continental counterparts feared was about to be set so destructively into motion.

"It will ruin us, and that is all we yet know, Mr. Holmes," the police superintendent, a Monsieur Albert Floquet, *Directeur Général de la Police Nationale*, confessed, upon our arrival, echoing the statement his colleagues had made in London. "And the ax is about to fall."

We had met with him in his grand office inside the *Prefecture de Police*, off Le Place Louis Lépine, on the Isle de Seine, all but in the shadows of Notre Dame itself, and he, who had, I observed, a glass eye in his left socket, confirmed:

"Chatter grows stronger, hinting the action is nearly at hand now, and some dread plot is afoot to undermine the nation, and do much harm."

Colonel Allard, who had traveled with us down from London, had tossed his callused hands toward the ceiling and lamented in gravely tones:

"Are we truly to be powerless before those who would assail the dignity of our very nation?"

After listening to that which these men had to tell by way of updates, Holmes had spoken:

"I can make you no promises in this matter save one," he had told this highest-ranking policeman, "that being that I shall do all that lies within my power to render France my aid."

"That is all that my country can fairly ask of you," Superintendent Floquet had agreed.

While the story of the adventure which followed that meeting is a tale worthy of its own narrative, one which I may or may not write of in due time, for now suffice to say that my friend outdid even himself, his courage absolute, and his deductions razor-keen, even in a city little known to him, and he soon uncovered an outrageous plot designed to throw France into a state of national emergency, concerned as it was with a villainous criminal cadre preparing to steal the body of Napoleon Bonaparte from *Les Invalides*, and hold it for the largest ransom ever demanded in the history of mankind: enough to cripple the economy for a year.

"Their plan was frankly one of genius as well as audacity," the detective was later to reveal to those officials who had brought him to the city, "and had I not been on-hand to bring it to a premature ending, I do not doubt it should have succeeded, for the explosives were in place, the get-away train in waiting, and the final stages of the criminals' preparations were complete. Instead they are bested, and for their efforts I doubt not theirs shall be a long and well-earned stay in prison."

"Upon Devil's Island, no less," Monsieur Floquet had vowed sternly. "But toward you, Monsieur Holmes, the gratitude of the Paris Police is without limits!"

"I think Monsieur President Grévy himself shall wish to pin upon you the *Légion d'honneuri!*"

The case was intended to remain shrouded in secrecy, but perhaps predictably the news leaked out so that by the day following the conspirators' apprehension it was the talk of the country, featured on the front pages of newspapers from Normandy to Nice, and Holmes found himself spoken of by Frenchmen everywhere, and hailed in the streets with ringing cries of:

"*C'est l'Anglais qui est le grand héros!*"

Not that Holmes readily embraced this celebrated status, for my friend, however much he might on occasion have enjoyed basking in the limelight of praise within the private sphere of his life, was one who recoiled from the extremes of exposure such fanfare brought, and by the following morning he had been in the process of planning our departure back to London after one last stroll about the delightful City of Light, the same walk in which I began this narrative on that lovely bridge over the Seine.

Though of course--*c'est la vie*--all his precise plans for homecoming were to be upended by the arrival at the luxurious Hôtel Meurice, where we had lodged, *gratis*, of one small and very determined young nun from a little convent in Normandy.

I do not think either of us shall ever forget her.

*****

She was waiting for Holmes in the vast and grand lobby of the famed hôtel, short and plain, but bright-eyed as a sparrow, and when we entered I saw her gaze focus upon my companion as she rose from a bench beside a stand of decorative palms, and advanced on him straight away.

"Holmes," I remarked, amused, "due to your recent fame here in the city, I think you are about to make the introduction of a religious sister."

His eyes, though, had already fallen upon the young woman, perhaps twenty-three by my estimation, so that he said merely:

"I perceive you are correct, Watson, and I observe that she who approaches is right-handed, reads often at night, may be slightly allergic to potatoes, is left-foot dominant in her stride, and I believe, resides in Normandy, where apple orchards are common. I also add that she is most gratified to encounter us here, and does so hardly by accident. I hazard that I may be about to acquire a client, whether I seek one or not."

As time did not permit me to ask how he deduced these facts, and from a distance, no less, I took them on faith.

Nevertheless, it was with a certain dignified cordiality that Holmes returned the petite nun's rather forward interception of him there in the lobby, and in reply to her statement in perfect English of--

"You are, I feel certain, Mr. Sherlock Holmes?"

--the detective said:

"I am indeed, Sister, and I deduce that though you are French, you acquired your fluency in my own language from persons native to the city of Coventry."

"Yes, sir," the young woman answered, "from a retired doctor and his wife, who were from that city, and later lived in a cottage near my family home, so that I grew up helping the lady with her gardening, and she found me an apt pupil in her efforts to teach me English. By the time I was ten she assured me I spoke it almost like a native."

"Ah, then I had it aright," Holmes said. "The rounded vowels of Coventry are distinct from those of most of the West Country, I have noted." He then added, "I intuit that the directness of your approach today is fueled by a circumstance of urgency, and do not think I am mistaken in noting that there is some matter about which you wish to speak to me?"

I wondered what could be so pressing in the orderly life of a nun, removed as it doubtless was from the turmoil of the outer world.

Not the least put off by my friend's directness, she confirmed:

"That is, indeed, a truth, sir. But I must not allow the gravity of my concerns to push aside all courtesy, so I will tell you, I am Sister Claire Ducasse, of Le Couvent des Saintes Pauline et Horsenthe."

"Yes, that is an eight-hundred-year-old convent northwest of the city, just inside the southernmost border of Normandy, I believe?"

"Yes, that is so," the small-statured nun agreed happily, her face lighting up. "It is a rural place, but quite lovely for all that. I might have known one with a reputation so profound as your own would have an awareness of our humble society there."

"The memorization of maps is rather a specialty of mine," Holmes granted.

"The wonders of Mr. Holmes' knowledge never fail to amaze me, either," I noted, offering this partner in mutual admiration my own smile.

"And I further perceive that you have only just stepped from the early-morning train which has brought you here," Holmes stated.

"That is so, yes," Sister Claire agreed, "I came into the hôtel only a moment before I saw the two of you enter as well. I think the timing of that was providential."

"Do you now?" said Holmes rhetorically.

As we had been having our conversation, brief though it had been to that point, in the hôtel lobby, Holmes made the suggestion:

"I think we should then proceed into the lounge area beyond the lobby proper, while I listen to what you have come some miles to tell me. I can only assume a religious sister does not hurry onto a train and then rush across a great city to locate a detective without there being some significant cause motivating her actions."

And this we did, our trio going into a formal but exceedingly comfortable chamber just off the ornate lobby, where after waiting for the young religious to be seated, we ourselves settled in, and Holmes was preparing to invite her to go on with her account, when, quite in character I would soon learn, the forward-natured Sister Claire seized the initiative and went straight into her tale with a rapid stream of words, saying:

"There has been a most dreadful theft from among us, which we discovered just before sunup at our morning mass, and I convinced Mother, er, that is our Mother Superior, Sister Benoîte being her name, to send me after you, rather than going for the police in our village."

"The police have not been informed?" I inquired.

"Having recently heard, even within our convent, of the reputation of Mr. Holmes, I thought it best to suggest it be to him that we take our grievance," she told me, "as the theft is one which pains our very souls, one and all."

"And why is that you have come instead of the Mother, herself?" Holmes pressed.

"Mother seldom leaves our walls."

"And so she elected to send you in her stead rather than a more senior from among your community?" I asked.

"She says I am a level-headed and quick-witted person," the sister revealed with neither modesty nor hesitation, simply stating this as a truth, "and so confesses she has come to rely upon my judgment, despite my comparatively tender years."

"I see," said Holmes, and at these words I caught a twinkle of mirth in his eyes.

"And as I go each day from our convent into the nearby town to teach art to the children at *les ecole*, she knows I hear more concerning the outer world and its affairs than do most of my sisters who are more resident within the convent itself."

"There it is then," Holmes said, his trace of faint amusement now openly displayed.

"Thus I learned in recent days of your success in foiling the shameful plot to purloin our late emperor in his casket, and when I told her of your much-praised capabilities, she gave me her consent to proceed at once as I have, here to Paris, catching the first train, and not stopping even for my breakfast."

Hearing this, I motioned for a waiter to bring us tea and croissants, with butter and fig jam, and a small wedge of brie dusted with basil, and this done I explained:

"At the very least we can offer you some refreshment while you give Mr. Holmes the entirety of your report."

She thanked me for this courtesy, and for his part Holmes opined:

"There was no counter-argument offered in favour of summoning the local police onto the scene of this crime, when time is always of the essence in a matter of theft?"

Sister Claire told him:

"In a convent all decisions are made by the Mother Superior rather than by committee, so her word was most final. Thus I had only to convince her."

"I see," the detective granted.

"I think," said Sister Claire, "that you are more capable than those well-meaning but little-experienced *gendarmerie* of the countryside, for all that they are good at heart, and as they all possess families within town, there would be much spreading of gossip regarding our misfortune, when I believe you are a man who practices the art of discretion, yes?"

"I am," Holmes concurred.

I thought of the truth there, for though over the years I had been party to many cases in which promises of secrecy bound us never to speak of them, I was likewise aware Holmes had been involved in still more delicate problems which he had never revealed, even to me, bound as he was in those instances by confidences secured by his word of honour. Thus, perhaps I should note that it was only with the Mother Superior's permission that I come to write of this tale some years after it transpired.

"And being that this is a shameful and shocking matter we are facing," Sister Claire told him, "it is the wish of Mother that no news of our misfortune escape, for a convent must above all do whatever is required to maintain its reputation as a place of order and holy conduct."

"And what is it that has been stolen?" I asked.

"Oh, in my rush I have not mentioned this, have I?" the little sister fussed, placing a hand over her heart and shaking her head in reproach.

Somehow she reminds me of someone I know, I reflected, *but I cannot think of whom.* (It would in fact be some time before I identified the resemblance.)

Just then the waiter, a tall and expressionless man, reminiscent of many a butler I had encountered, returned with our tray, and I leaned over to serve our guest before myself, and as I did, she thanked me, before revealing at last:

"What was stolen, Mr. Holmes, is a much-treasured altar cross, a gift to our convent from the Countess d'Arnois many centuries ago. It is not as valuable as perhaps its august history makes it sound, but it is dear to us all in our sisterhood, for having rested atop the altar for each mass said in our chapel for generations, and during the terrors of the Revolution my antecedents in holy life hid it from bad men who would have seized relics, and melted them down in order to fund their wars. It is said some of my preceding sisters of that age even endured the roughness of soldiers who intruded within our walls seeking to loot what they could find there, yet never gave up the cross' whereabouts."

"I can see then why this item would be so valuable to you all," I offered up, thinking of the centuries it had rested in this Norman convent.

"Yes," Sister Claire confirmed, "I do not doubt one could reap a fair return were it to be sold for its metal, and its stones."

"Concerning this theft, I need to know the details, if you please," Holmes said imperiously, but with courtesy and obvious interest.

"Then I must begin my relation of this dreadfulness some two nights ago," the sister stated, "for it was then, amid the rural darkness and behind the thick walls of our old convent, that there began events that surely relate to this crime discovered just before dawn today. I am a light sleeper as a rule, and it has long been my ability, or my misfortune, to come awake at the slightest noise that does not fit itself into what is normal in my surroundings. And on that night, perhaps an hour and a half after we had all risen together and assembled in the chapel to pray Matins, so by then about three in the morning, let us say, I was stirred from a nebulous dream by the sound of movement in the outer passageway just beyond the small room I occupy with my bed and writing table within."

"You say it was two nights ago that you first discerned odd sounds in the darkness, yet the theft only occurred this morning?" Holmes asked her.

"Yes," she confirmed.

"And what precisely did you hear?"

"It was the noise of someone moving in the passageway, with an attempt at stealth. I might have ignored it, for it is not absolutely forbidden for one of us to leave our cells under some conditions, but I testify I have learned to recognize the distinct sound of the shoes we nuns of Saintes Pauline et Horsenthe wear, made in town by the cobbler, Monsieur Tremblay, and also the individual footfalls of the twelve sisters who reside with me on the north side of the convent, and these footsteps were unknown to my ears."

"You have learned the footfalls of those familiar to you?" Holmes said, impressed. "Then the Mother Superior is correct to judge you quick-witted and observant. Pray, go on."

"Wait," I interjected, "you say you know the footfalls of those cloistered sisters who reside with you in the *north* wing, but there are those who sleep elsewhere?"

"Yes, for while we who are young in years and with a lesser time in holy orders, sleep along the larger north end of the convent, those older sisters who hold some office, sleep on the smaller south side, in that wing."

"Ah," I noted. "Thank you."

"Who are these who sleep to the south?" Holmes asked her.

"The cellarer, Sister Jeanne, the choir mistress, Sister Odile, and Sister Rodanne, our disciplinarian, who is charged with gently seeing all rules are followed. Also Sister Radegund, the alms-mistress, who gives charity to the poor, Sister Remi the infirmarian, who acts as our druggist and nurse in minor matters. And of course Mother, herself, in the smallest room."

The smallest out of humility, I judged.

"So six there in that southern wing of the building," Holmes said in summary.

"Yes, sir, that is correct, eighteen of us in total. Twice as many junior as senior."

"Very good, pray continue," said the detective.

"So all within the order there are known to me," she said, "and I have learned my fellow residents of the north wing by sound of their movements alone, but these footsteps I heard in the night I did not know. Could it somehow be Sister Rodanne, I wondered, checking that all were in their rooms, an action which I had rarely known her to take? But what truly drew my ear was that rather than moving with the confident stride of one who had legitimate reason to pass openly through the darkness, these footfalls were of one seeking to progress in a stealthy fashion, for there was a cushioned, wispy noise as of one on tiptoes. Also beyond this there was something off with the steps themselves, as if the person limped, or dragged a limb, and none of us in the convent possesses such a deformity."

"That is frightening," I said, reflecting on how it must have been unnerving to lie in the dark and hear this just beyond one's door: a door which was surely kept unlocked.

"It roused more of a sense of curiosity in me, I suppose," she testified.

"I tell you, Watson," Holmes noted to me, "this young woman does impress me, recognizing the distinction of a tiptoed step over a normal stride. Can you, Sister, describe the noise you heard the footfalls making, perhaps demonstrating the pacing by replicating them thusly here?"

Sister Claire paused a moment in thought, then, even as she remained seated, used her own tiptoed feet to imitate a stumbling, uneven, step, with a lengthy interval between to represent stealth.

"There was that much time between each pace?" Holmes asked, his brow furrowed in thought.

"Yes, about as long," she answered, "for each individual motion was slow."

"Interesting, indeed," Holmes said with an odd tone in his words, and I saw he had raised an eyebrow for a moment before settling it back again.

"So hearing this," I said, "you, of course, intuited there was something odd?"

"Most assuredly odd," she admitted, "for there was both a sneaky aspect and an awkward one, as if with an infirmity, and thus I rose in silence and went to my door and listened with my ear pressed against it, and believe I heard this quiet movement farther-on by then, down the passageway, so I risked cracking open my door in the quietest fashion, and peered out, but in the lightlessness of the night there was nothing to be seen, not even a candle-flame being carried, as one should think there would be, and I heard no more footsteps, either because whosoever was walking was by then too far away for my ears to discern, or, and this is disconcerting to ponder, because the person had somehow apprehended the opening of my door, and had frozen mid-step, hiding in the darkness."

This last suggestion felt decidedly eerie to me as well, and I did not envy her being alone as she had been, staring down into un-dispelled blackness of a country night.

"What was your next course of action?" asked Holmes.

"I was bold enough to stay there in that pose, listening for…some indefinable time, two minutes, I might guess, were I to estimate, and I looked and I reached outward with my hearing, but discerned nothing else, and never saw anything at all, so I closed my door, feeling an uneasiness in my instincts."

"I think that is altogether understandable," I said.

"You felt 'unease', as you describe it, but not a sense of fear?" Holmes asked her.

"As a rule I do attempt to be courageous in this temporal life," she answered him, "for ultimately all lies in God's hands."

She is a true believer in the teachings of her faith, I thought.

"Tell me of the rest of the night," Holmes urged her.

"In absolute darkness I went and sat upon my bed, conscious that what I had heard suggested few logical explanations. I stayed as quiet as I could and waited to see if I discerned this particular sister returning, yet this person never did pass by again, and as I finally grew sleepy, I began to wonder if the entire matter could have been a dream within a half-slumbering state."

"A possibility," I concurred. "Have you had moments of sleep-walking or lucid slumber in the past?"

"I have not," she told me, "for though a light sleeper, I am generally an untroubled one."

Here Holmes said:

"Even beyond the later reality of the theft of the cross in today's pre-dawn, I think you had reason to believe this incident was not a dream?"

"Yes, quite so," Sister Claire agreed. "The next morning, you see, all my sisters were present at the chapel service and later at table, and though I carefully asked if their slumber had been disturbed in such a way that had them leave their rooms in the night, none said that it had. Though still puzzled, I went on into town and taught water-colours to some little girls at the academy there, and the longer I progressed into day, the less real the puzzling scenario of the night seemed. With time I could almost have laid it aside and forgotten it altogether as a meaningless oddity, I think."

"And yet...?" Holmes prodded.

"And yet the next night, at about the same time, I again snapped awake from an uneasy slumber, jarred by the sound of more footsteps in the passageway."

"Good heavens," I breathed at these unsettling tidings, "the unidentified person was back?"

"No, Doctor," Sister Claire said, her eyes going round, "for instantly my ears told me that though out in the hallway, just beyond my door, a person was certainly moving as slowly and cautiously as had been the case the night before, this was not the same individual."

More frightful still, this news! I thought.

"And how did you know it was a different party?" Holmes asked, with truest curiosity, I could tell.

"Though this second soul who disturbed the late hours was likewise moving with exceeding care to make as little sound as possible, just as whoever had been out there the previous night, these footfalls were more regular, devoid the limp. I do not think I had ever heard this stride before then. There was something *violating* about it."

"I say again, you have remarkable talents," said Holmes, impressed.

"I listened," she said, "and waited, considering whether I should go out to see if all was well, and was still occupied in this dilemma when within seconds the *next* footsteps moved stealthily down the hallway, likewise coming from that same direction in passing my door. These told of a motion that was swifter than the last had been a moment before, and were so quiet that I barely heard them save as.... I can only note that they were as a deeper silence within the nighttime silence itself."

A very strange description, thought I. Thus I asked:

"A second person inexplicably out in the night within minutes of the first? Three in all over two nights' time?"

"Yes," she answered with directness. "The night before, one party had been moving quite alone in the dark hallway, sounding as if a leg were slightly dragged behind it, and last night, or rather in the pre-dawn of this morning, perhaps three-thirty, I believe it was, I heard two different people in the outer hall, each proceeding quietly. I recognized that the sound of the second footfalls of last night, the third and final party, in other words, matched that of someone from the convent, for beyond knowing the cobbler's shoes, I had often heard this stride on other occasions."

"When was that?" I inquired.

"In the normal course of daily life, when all were gathered together for prayers, or for our meals. As it was not a junior, I began to concentrate my thoughts, and judged that from among the seniors only Mother's stride alone was I able to identify upon hearing it, so I knew it was not she, but it was still a senior from among the sisters who was then out in the hall, for what purpose I could not envision."

"And how did you receive this realization that, eliminating

your Mother Superior from consideration, it was one of five older women?"

"Somehow this reassured me," she said, "as I thought there must have been a legitimate purpose in what I heard, for with so many years in holy orders, the seniors among our community are trusted to the highest degree, and hold the most important positions."

I understood her sentiment, for though brought up Scots-Presbyterian, my impression was that Roman Catholic nuns were as a rule dedicated and pious.

"But even the mollifying fact the footfalls were those of one of the older among us," she continued, "made me feel puzzlement, for all that I trusted there must have been some reason for her movement through the night."

"I dare say it did," I agreed.

"What was your next action upon making this quasi-identification?" Holmes asked her.

"Had it been one of my fellow younger sisters from there on the north side, I could have told you whom it was by the very sound, and if it had been one of my peers, I may have gone out to her and asked if she were well. Though if my impulse the first night was to open my door, last night some inner caution held me back, and all at once I felt a most distinct sense of fear."

"You at last felt fear?" Holmes pressed her.

"Decidedly," she said, "for though I trust in God's protection, I am but human, and it was no sense of superstitious dread I felt take hold, but a true instinctive testimony from within myself that I should not interrupt the sound of these movements by intruding upon them. For if I did...."

She lifted a hand out before her, indicating uncertainty.

"Probably a wise decision," I told her.

"And yet I wish I had," she told me. "For then upon that second night I would have known whatever the answer was to this rising mystery, and by knowing could perhaps have changed the course of what was to come to pass in our convent so soon after."

"It is far more likely that misfortune should have befallen you," I judged.

"That would have been in God's hands," she said softly, though I also saw she was only too conscious of the truth of my words.

Here, though I sat back in my chair and asked:

"I find myself slightly puzzled, Sister, for it seems clear that whatever their reputation for sanctity might be, whoever from among the senior members of your convent was in the passageway likely involved herself in the theft of the gold altar cross before dawn this morning. Why would you not inform the local police of what you heard, so that they might interview the small pool of suspects, five in number, you say, rather than you making a journey to Paris to consult with Sherlock Holmes in the face of such weighty evidence?"

Undeterred by my words, Sister Claire shook her head and said:

"You must indulge me by waiting for the rest of my account, Doctor," she said, "as matters indeed grow stranger."

"Stranger still?" I marveled.

"Oh, yes," she maintained.

At this Holmes nodded and said:

"Patience, my dear Watson. If you would please continue, Sister?"

"After a time, perhaps a half an hour, maybe slightly longer, despite my trepidations, curiosity became dominant, and I did indeed leave my cell in the darkness, and passed down the hallway, retracing the path taken by whomever from among the senior sisters had crept by me. I went down the spiraling stairway at the passageway's end, and came to be in the choir loft of the chapel, some twenty feet above the sanctuary, and there I froze, startled, for in this sanctified space, I saw two things which puzzled me."

"What were these?" I inquired.

"Down upon the chapel floor, so old that the steps of those of our order assembling for mass have worn them to smoothness over time, lighted as the air was by the flickering of votive candles in their red glass holders, I saw the beautiful old cross was gone from the altar, and also espied a sister, whom I could not identify, for her back was to me and her face covered, standing before the altar itself, holding a canvas sack of about a meter in length."

"A-ha," I burst out, "so she was witnessed by you red-handed, in the act of purloining the cross!"

"No," said Sister Claire.

"No?" I challenged, startled.

"In saying, Doctor," she explained, "that I caught her 'red-handed' a metaphor I incidentally do understand for all that I am French, you are not correct, for it was not an act of theft, I beheld."

"The cross was gone, you say, and yet you were not at that instant a witness to its theft?" I demanded, uncomprehending.

Holmes said to me:

"You see how your assumptions have lead you to err, Watson, thus do allow the good sister's testimony to unfold as it will."

"Not theft, no, sir," Sister Claire answered, "for I tell you instead, this person was not stealing the cross, she was in fact taking it out from the sack she carried, and was with movements of gentle reverence, replacing it upon the altar."

"What?" I asked, taken aback. "She was *returning* the cross to the altar?"

"Yes, Doctor, doing exactly that. I watched as she set it into its time-honoured place, from which it had been absent when first I looked down, then she genuflected and crossed herself, and stepped out from the chapel and back toward the cloisters of the seniors, in the south wing."

"That seems utterly inexplicable," I said.

Giving no commentary, Holmes asked:

"What were your actions in the aftermath of what you had just witnessed?"

"I waited a number of minutes," she answered, "but saw no one else, and heard nothing whatsoever around me, so I slipped down into the chapel and went to the altar, genuflecting and crossing myself in this holy place, as had my predecessor, and I looked closely at the relic."

"I am glad to hear it, for doubtless your thoughts turned to..."

Here Holmes paused, and I realized he was testing her.

"My thoughts turned to whether the cross was genuine, or whether I had witnessed some switch being affected, the treasured relic for a counterfeit one."

"A-ha!" said Holmes, pleased. "Perfect! You were right to think along such lines, though I take it you satisfied yourself that it was the same item, and not a forgery?"

"It was the same cross," stated the nun, "that had always sat there, and no replica, for I knew it in the most minute detail, from having stared reverently toward it in thousands of hours of masses over the five years of my time in the order, and I saw that it had been set with such precision onto the fine white cloth that covered the altar that it rested exactly within a little ring that over time its weight had made on the cloth's surface."

"An impressive feat of observation," said Holmes, "especially in the mid-hours of night, alone in a heightened state of nervousness, with only candlelight filtered through red votive-glass to aid you."

"I had to know, and next to this my fears counted for little."

Still, it sounded to me like she was lucky, I thought.

"There was no sign to be had," continued Sister Claire, "that the cross had ever been absent, though the once-empty altar-top testified that it had been removed at some point in the time between Matins, when we as a group assembled after midnight to pray, and my looking on at its return nearly four hours later, yet I had witnessed it had been taken by someone. I had no idea what all this could mean, and found it an overwhelming assault on my senses."

"Yes, I can see why that was," I reassured her.

"What did you do in the immediate sense after this episode?" Holmes asked, pressing on.

"I began to think upon the fact I had heard two parties moving in the hallway before I came down, yet had only seen one of them, the senior sister who had returned the cross, and grew frightened by the thought that it was possible this other party was waiting in the darkness of the stairs, or the hall outside my room. It took all the courage I could find within me to go, then, back up to my cell."

"You made it there without incident, I take it?" I asked her.

"Thankfully, yes, I encountered no one else in my trip back upstairs to my room, where I sat thinking through it all, sleep an impossibility. Finding no answers, I prayed God give me clarity, but this He did not grant, and no matter how deeply I considered them, the facts merely brought rise to more questions. Whom had I heard the first night shuffling past, almost like a cripple, and of the pair I had heard an hour before, one a nun, the other unidentified, who were they, and what was the purpose of their sneaking along in the nighttime? Above all I wondered whom had I seen below me in the chapel? Why was the cross taken, and why was it returned, and by whom? Nothing made the slightest sense, and no scenario I could engineer explained all factors at play."

"Why did you not go at once and report these events to your superior?" Holmes asked. "For I hazard from the facts that you did not."

"It is true, I did not," Sister Claire said, and her face showed both regret and a trace of shame. "I fully intended to in the morning, but in the last hours of night I held back because in my vanity I believed if I pondered hard enough there in my room, I could perceive the truth of things, and take the solution to the mystery to Mother when I made my report."

"For that matter," I inquired, "you have said you are entirely satisfied it was not the Mother Superior you saw in the chapel, putting the cross back onto the empty altar, but is this something you still hold to with utter certainty?"

"I knew it was not she, Doctor," said Sister Claire, "not only because the footfalls were not her own, but also for the reason that I saw the figure in the chapel, whoever she was, lift her right arm far out before her and place the cross onto the altar, and Mother has had somewhat limited use of that limb since an accident before she came to holy orders. To see Mother extend that arm is to see a slowness in the action, one which I know brings her pain."

"There you have it, Watson," said Holmes. "And you see how precisely observant our young visitor is? I salute you, Sister, on your keenness of eye and the analytical state of your mind. Do not feel unduly troubled that you have as yet failed to solve this puzzle, for even I, with all the acumen of my training and long experience, cannot as yet say what truly occurred."

"I thank you for sparing my feelings," the sister replied, "but I know I am, guilty of errors."

"You have said the cross is currently missing," I reminded her. "So despite your having seen it returned to the altar just before four in the morning, it is also true that at dawn or a little before, the cross *was* ultimately found to be gone from the chapel, and the convent grounds?"

"That is so," agreed Sister Claire. "It is missing and we know not where."

"Is there…." I continued, "some legitimate reason the cross would have been taken down from the altar in the night, some ritual, perhaps, that might explain why the elder nun was seen restoring it to its place? If so maybe her actions are wholly unrelated to its disappearance."

"'Disappearance'? It is *theft*, Watson," Holmes corrected me.

"No, Doctor Watson," she answered adamantly, "there is no ritual of that sort in our order, for the cross has its place atop the altar, where it had sat for generations."

"Then the mind leaps," said I, "to a suspicion that the cross had been stolen not once but twice, and the nun you espied in the night somehow recovered it after the first incident and restored it to its rightful place. Clearly she was unable to prevent the second crime, and has not, for whatever reasons, spoken up concerning her involvement the first recovery."

It was a fanciful notion, I knew, but it was one that had leapt out fully-formed from my brain.

"To be certain these facts do raise many possibilities," Sherlock Holmes said, "thus tell me, Sister, who in the hour of dawn first discovered the cross to be missing, and under what circumstances?"

"It was when we were progressing into the chapel for the adoration of the Blessed Sacrament, which we do each morning at the start of our day. All at once, in our double line of progression, we saw as one that the altar was barren of its most precious decoration, and the realization imposed a profound effect upon us all."

"Or all save one, I suspect," Holmes noted drily. "What, then, followed this discovery?"

"There was consternation and confusion so profound that it raised an outcry, dispelling our usual silence in the morning chapel, and I gazed around me and noted that upon every face this seemed the same genuine reaction, no one I saw seemed to be creating an ersatz dismay, and after a long moment of this, Mother, who herself approached the altar, genuflected and made the sign of the cross, examined the surroundings, and only then did she turn back to the rest of us, all seventeen in number, and declared that we must not let this happening prevent us from fulfilling our holy duties, and thus we undertook the service of adoration of Our Lord's presence, and only after this did she usher us to the refectory, where the rule of non-communication barely contained us in our collective wish to cry out in dreadful horror that so ancient a thing, which stood almost as the very emblem of our convent, was no longer with us."

"And then?" asked Holmes.

"Then there was a gathering in the front hall, and we were each called to Mother's office and questioned as to whether we had seen or heard anything. Only then did I tell my tale, and to my shame Mother let her head fall into her hands at my tidings, and she asked why I had not woken her at once, and I gave my reasons, weak though they were, and only half understood by me."

"What did she say?" I asked, infusing my question with sympathy.

"In short, that my sin was one of vanity in believing I might, myself, lend understanding to what was proven beyond me. Had I brought these facts to her attention, the theft--the second theft-- may have been prevented."

There came then a brief pause in the narrative, even as

around us the daily life of the hôtel went on, contrasting the tale of a convent in the country, and the stark events that had transpired there in the silence of night.

At last Sister Claire said:

"Mother told me that was that then, the police must be made aware of the crime, and come take my statement. I, however, had gone into town each day, you remember, and had been hearing much talk of recent events in Paris, and of the remarkable Englishman, Mr. Sherlock Holmes, and of what he--that is to say what you, sir--have done for France."

Holmes flashed a small self-aware smile, and nodded.

"I told Mother of how you were the talk of the capital, your name on all lips, it seemed, and told her I might rectify any harm I had done by my silence, if I had her blessing to go into Paris and find you, for I felt certain then, as I still hope now, that you will come to the aid of we women in our rural home, bereft of a treasure so dear to our hearts. And so she sent me this same morning on the first train, and as you saw, thanks to God, I found you."

"How *did* you find him?" I asked. "Paris is not a small place."

A light came on in the little nun's eyes, and with a bashful smile she allowed:

"I thought through the matter on the train down from Normandy, you see. I knew there were likely but a handful of hôtels where a gentleman such as Mr. Holmes, and you, of course, Doctor, might be staying, and rather than visit each in turn, I went to the one person I knew who would certainly be informed on this subject."

"Who was that?" I inquired, my brow wrinkled with curiosity. "A policeman?"

"Why a street child, of course," Sister Claire answered.

At this Holmes emitted a barking laugh of profound

approval and said:

"Watson, this person impresses me at every turn with her acumen, for as you know I have long availed myself of the all-knowing awareness of those children who reside on the streets."

"Your Irregulars," I agreed, putting his collective name onto them.

"Sister Claire," Holmes said, looking toward her now with admiration and a settled certainty, "I find you a woman perspicacious beyond your years, your intellect in no way muted by the shelter of the convent in which you dwell. Yes, I shall certainly return with you to Normandy, and see what I might do toward the recovery of your order's treasure."

"Oh, Mr. Holmes, I do thank you!" the nun gushed. "I held it as a matter of faith in my heart that you would, and prayed most ardently for such a reply to my entreaties. Even so, to receive it is most gratifying!"

"I caution you, though," Holmes felt honour-bound to tell her, "a stolen item is not often to be easily recovered, and I confess, I am out of my element in the French countryside, whereas back in London I might even now have an insight into where the cross was taken, and by whom."

"Ah, but I hold every confidence in you," Sister Claire told him, "and know if anyone can set this matter right, and redeem me for the faults which rose from my own rôle in the scenario, it is you, sir."

"Then let us go to Normandy at once!" Holmes cried, raising himself from the chair and setting off straightaway for the hôtel door, leaving Sister Claire, and myself as usual, to hurry after him, our fine little breakfast tray abandoned in our wake.

*****

We were shortly on a train to Normandy, Paris being a place

where railroad lines converged on a scale rivaling even London, and since the convent sat near the very border of that county which had featured so importantly in Britain's past, our journey was but a brief one. As we passed toward the northwest through countryside that reminded me of the south of England, Holmes, who had been ruminating on the facts as related to him by Sister Claire, broke his silence when he asked:

"Tell me of the doors to the convent and chapel. They are, I would presume, locked each evening?"

"Precisely so," Sister Claire answered. "It is a nightly ritual, Mother, who wears the keys to all buildings on a chain at her waist, goes and checks the doors and windows herself each night, always in the company of a novice sister, so that she might not only aid her, but bear witness that all is done as required. The nights when I heard the footsteps, and which later saw our cross taken, were no exceptions."

"I see," said Holmes, "and there are no other entryways into the buildings save the doors themselves?"

"None known to me," she replied, "though I suppose a skilled burglar could always find some manner of ingress."

"That is their great talent," I concurred.

"The convent is old in the extreme," Holmes said, "dating, I believe, to the age of the Conqueror himself, so it is entirely possible that in a place so steeped in antiquity, there might be certain passages that lie little-known, or even long-forgotten."

"That, I suppose, must be considered true," the nun concurred, "though the question then must arise that if these are beyond the knowledge of we who dwell within Saintes Pauline et Horsenthe, how would they be known to an outsider?"

"A valid point," it was agreed by the detective, "but in my investigation I must consider such unlikely possibilities. As it was erected during the Middle Ages, I presume there is a crypt to be found below the church itself?"

"Oh, yes, an ancient one," Sister Claire said at once, "but unused for centuries. For many generations it has been within the little cemetery down the lane where we sisters have been laid to rest while we await Judgment Day. We pray there the third Friday of each month, and upon the morning of the Feast of All Souls, asking forgiveness for the deceased."

"That falls upon November the first, I believe?" I said.

"Just the same," I was answered. "And there I have seen graves dating to the late 1500s, so I think the chapel undercroft has not been in use since then."

Our companion is quite the historian, I thought.

"Nonetheless," Holmes judged, "should I require access to the crypts, would access be made available to me?"

"That only Mother would know," the young nun said almost meekly, "but I am certain if it is at all possible, she should accommodate you, for she is desirous of the cross' return."

"I can imagine," I spoke up.

Sister Claire turned her eyes downward and I saw some strong emotion pass through her, as did Holmes, and I asked:

"Are you entirely well, Sister?"

"It is just," she confessed, "that mention of Mother brings to mind how I failed her in my reticence to speak up concerning those sounds of passage I heard on the last two nights. She is the kindest of women, for all the authority she holds, and has always been good to me, yet I know I have profoundly disappointed her in this regard."

"Take heart, then," Holmes said to her with a kindness in his words, "for you have brought me onto this case, and ere this matter is concluded, that may well redeem you in your superior's regard."

Sister Claire smiled, not so much at Holmes as into space itself, and quietly said:

"I do pray that shall be so."

*****

We arrived by mid-afternoon at a small country depot in the community beyond the convent, and I found it a cheerful and thoroughly pleasant place, this Norman town. There were cobbles upon its main street, which was lined with neat little houses, nearly all with a shoppe of some kind on the lowest floor, providing whatever goods the locals required. Even the horses pulling the carts around us seemed content with their lot, and the men driving them were tanned by the sun, with cordiality in their eyes, most with fragrant tobacco pipes clenched in their mouths.

Through this scene of bucolic tranquility, it was but a short walk to the grounds of the nunnery itself down a well-travelled path, where the dirt underfoot was of an almost yellow shade of brown, and the steeple of the convent church became visible almost as soon as we stepped beyond the limits of the town proper.

"The farms, if you note, Watson," said Holmes, "do vary from those in England, where the families who work them live amid the same acreage they sow, but here in the north of France, the farmers reside in town, and go out each day to tend their fields, and then return."

"That explains the fact that so many wagons are heading out from town toward the farms," I observed.

"Yes, the workers shall be going out again after coming in for their mid-day meal," Sister Claire informed us.

"I understand," said I, "that hereabouts the main meal of the day is served at noon rather than evening as it is in England."

"A better arrangement, ours, if I may say so," Sister Claire added, and from a medical standpoint I had to agree, thinking of how many of my patients complained of bedtime indigestion following a hearty eight o' clock supper.

We reached the open gates of the convent, formed of wrought iron, tall and black and well-tended despite what I had no doubt was a considerable age, and fell in walking behind she who had brought us to this quiet and inviting spot in the Norman countryside. The largest of the buildings was, I saw, constructed of neatly-cut gray stone, well-worn by the weather of many generations, moss in the crevices here and there, adding something to its beauty.

Now this, I thought, *is how a French convent should look.*

We were taken down a hallway to the open door of a large office, just outside of which stood a plaster statue of a female saint, her face in stark ecstasy despite the arrows which pierced her heart. Here Sister Claire cleared her throat and announced humbly:

"Mother, I have returned with the English gentlemen."

"Then you have made excellent time," came the reply.

The woman behind the desk rose, her habit black, her head-covering stark white in contrast, and I saw she was tall in height, and thin, and as we had been told, one of her arms contained a stiffness in its movements as she gestured for us all to come inside. Her eyes, each the colour of a green olive, were worried, I noted, and she frowned before nodding formally to each of us, and then shutting her office door.

She said in English:

"I thank you, Sister Claire, and you most particularly, gentlemen. I do welcome you both to the convent of Saints Pauline and Horsenthe, where Godliness is pursued, and nothing of the nature of the theft about which I sent Sister Claire to tell you, has ever transpired across our order's long past."

Holmes joined me in bowing to this senior-most nun, and then he said:

"She has made us aware of the loss of a relic long possessed by this religious house, and also informed us of the circumstances of its theft, which occurred sometime in the latter part of the overnight hours, between perhaps four AM and dawn."

"Yes, that is sadly correct," said the Mother Superior, shaking her head and giving every impression of feeling truly bereft at the loss. "Has she also told you of the fact she discerned movement in the nights prior to the actual crime, yet did not speak to me of hearing these?"

I felt a stab of pity for Sister Claire, to have her omission brought up so soon, when I knew it shamed her.

"This she freely confessed to me," Holmes said, too neutrally to convey disapproval. "And also of seeing a nun, unidentified by her, returning the cross shortly before it went missing with greater finality."

"Then you have it," Mother Superior agreed, sighing.

She seemed to pull herself back from some inner reflection, and said:

"I fear the weight of these troubles has dulled my sense of propriety and manners. Pray, Mr. Sherlock Holmes, Dr. John Watson, do be seated."

At that Sister Claire, from beside us, moved to pull out chairs for us, though she did not take one herself, merely stood meekly at the wall behind us, and it was only after we had sat that Mother returned to her own seat.

"Your fee will be paid regardless of the outcome, I assure you, Mr. Holmes," Mother went on, "but I will ask you, is there the slightest hope of seeing our precious cross returned to us, given that the thief has had a head start of many hours?"

"There is always hope," Holmes stated, "and to that end,

may I ask, Mother, have I your permission to go where I must on these grounds, and may I speak to whomever I need to question, or are there restrictions which the propriety of religious life must of necessity impose upon my work?"

A fair question, I thought, as we came from a predominantly Protestant country, and did not wish to unintentionally give offense to those who hosted us here.

"You have my leave," answered the Mother Superior, "to conduct yourself as you see fit, to go anywhere within these grounds you require, and to speak to any you wish, for though we have only met this moment, I believe you to be gentlemen of principle and discretion, and you shall each enjoy my trust."

Holmes bowed his head with what looked to be genuine humility, aware, I didn't doubt, of the magnitude of the favour being bestowed upon us, for as a rule, a convent was not an environment where a man would have such freedom of access.

"I thank you for that trust, Mother," he said. "My friend and I shall do our best not to abuse it in any manner."

The Mother nodded and adjusted her spectacles upon her vast Gallic nose.

"Now," Holmes began, and I saw a shift in him from guest to investigator, his tone deepening as well, "I must ask you, have you any intonation of by whom this cross was taken, or why? Is there any information you might have withheld from general knowledge here within your community which you might at this time confide to me?"

"I know nothing, alas," she stated, "and there is little else I can add, however much I wish that I could do so. I know only that the cross was in its place when we gathered after midnight for the vigil of Matins, and that it was gone when we assembled once more at Lauds, to pray before breaking our fast in the first light of morning, at Prime. Beyond that I have only the sorrowful knowledge I came to hold quite late in matters concerning what

Sister Claire tells me she heard last night and the night which came before, that being the unexplained movement of apparently two to three separate souls, one possibly a sister in this convent."

Or wearing the footwear of one, I reflected, pondering again the oddity of this claim.

Saying nothing about this, Holmes went on:

"Sister Claire tells me there is an undercroft below the church. Is the space talked of among the community here?"

"Talked of?" Mother asked.

"Is it referred to?" Holmes clarified. "Is its existence much known?"

"It is universally known," said Mother, "but I cannot think it rests often in the thoughts of any of us here, as it is kept closed off."

"Is it possible I could visit this space?" Sherlock Holmes asked.

Without replying directly, Mother removed a key from a chain at her waist and passed it across, and only then did she say:

"I must warn you Mr. Holmes, the undercroft with its burials of our sister-forebears of long ago, has not been used in some indefinable time, nor has the door itself been opened in three years. If you are thinking the area could have been used as a hiding place for the miscreants who purloined our cross, I think that unlikely, especially as from within there is no door to the outside, and the only one that does exist is stoutly locked, and the key remains ever in my possession."

"Yes, my thoughts *have* gone to the possibility that the crypt was used to access the church," Holmes agreed.

"I will leave that for you to confirm," Mother stated.

"For what reason was it opened three years ago?" I asked.

"I ordered my sisters to assemble with me there in prayer," she replied.

I saw some hesitation on her part to say more, yet Holmes did not let this pass.

"You have assembled there only on this singular occasion three years ago?" he pushed.

I noted from the corner of my eye that Sister Claire, behind me but still within my peripheral sight, slightly altered her expression, and her eye betrayed a trace of some tell-tale thought, though she kept her face solemn in the presence of the Mother, who was, I detected a most serious sort of person.

I saw Holmes had likewise caught this change in the young nun's countenance, as he turned to her and said:

"You, perhaps, had a thought, Sister?"

Before replying, Claire looked toward her superior, who gave her a faint nod.

"I am sorry," said the young nun, "I did not mean to contribute my own thoughts into the discussion concerning the reason for the undercroft's unsealing three years ago, and should have had better control over myself."

"But as you did not, you may now answer the gentleman, Sister," Mother said, not with annoyance but with a certain mild disapproval.

"The reason the door was unlocked and Mother led us down into the crypt was to put to rest the talk that had arisen for several days before this event."

"Talk?" Holmes pressed, seizing on this with obvious interest.

Yet Sister Claire showed reluctance and some trace of what could have been embarrassment, and it was actually Mother who finished the explanation for her.

"The shameful truth, Mr. Holmes, is many among our order claimed to have heard noises coming up from that old place, sounds in the night that revived long dormant talk of the crypts being haunted."

"Oh, indeed!" Holmes spoke up. "And what noises were these?"

"The accounts differed," said Mother, "some hearing the sound of bumping and objects overturning, others the whispering of voices, always female. One of our order, Sister Madonna, claimed she heard her own voice calling out through the stones of the chapel floor, as if from a mimic, I suppose, and became hysterical. That was, as the saying goes, the final straw. I held no patience for such reports, and had heard nothing myself, nor I suspect did anyone else save a few who may have discerned perhaps rats living underground and moving about. I ordered all talk to cease, yet it did not, I find no gladness in reporting, and so I unlocked the door and led everyone below ground to show it was a harmless space, dark and filled with but cobwebs and the mortal remains of those who had once dwelled here long ago, no one to be frightened of in life or in death."

"A wise outlook," Holmes informed her, approving of her disdain for the preternatural.

"And after these prayers, did the sounds cease?" I, however, asked.

"The reports of them did," Mother told me. "Whether any noises ever truly existed beyond exaggerations and imaginings, I cannot judge."

I did not know what to think at this report, though I could not see how after a third of a decade it could be of relevance to the present-day theft in the night, yet I noted Holmes stood still for a long moment,

"Perhaps this episode has no bearing here," he said, "but I shall keep it in mind when I investigate the undercroft and its crypts. However, other courses of action come first."

"In the aforementioned immediate sense, then, what will you do now, Mr. Holmes?" Mother asked from behind the vastness of her desk, covered as it was in neat stacks of papers and several books, including a leather-bound missal of daily services.

"I shall investigate the chapel, as it is the site of this occurrence, and see where that might lead, perhaps into a direction I have not heretofore considered. And then, Mother, I ask that shortly after this you kindly assemble what Sister Claire has referred to as the seniors among those who reside here, for I would speak with them."

Mother nodded and said:

"It shall be so."

"Have the quarters of the sisters who reside here been searched?" Holmes put to the older woman.

"Searched?" Mother said back, a frown beginning upon her brow. "Why, no, as we live under a vow of poverty, it would benefit no sister here to steal the cross for monetary gain, if that is your implication."

This answer seemed to me both inadequate and the height of naiveté, and doubtless Holmes felt the same but only said:

"Perhaps, Mother, a search might be undertaken at this time, and the results reported to me?"

"I..." There was a struggle on the woman's face, before she said, "Very well, Sister Claire shall assist me in this distasteful action, though even were one of my sisters here, whom I trust to the utmost, to have been responsible for the cross' taking, surely a hundred hiding places suggest themselves rather than the guilty party implicating herself by leaving the item in her cell?"

"Nonetheless, Mother, I think it would be a wise action," Holmes insisted.

"Then, as I said, it shall be done," the Superior of the convent granted.

"My deepest thanks, Mother," Holmes said. "All that is preliminary having been addressed, I beg your permission to begin my own efforts."

"Then you have it," she replied. "And God be with you."

With that, Holmes rose and bowed with some solemnity to she who sat across from us, then we took our leave of the two nuns, one old and stern, the other young and vividly bright in her personality, and the case of the French convent was begun.

*****

As we walked slowly down the hall, toward where a where a wider passageway branched off in the direction of the chapel, I said to Holmes:

"Do you think I am correct in retaining the feeling that though Sister Claire is not at present in the Mother's best graces, overall she enjoys her superior's confidence?"

"I sense," said Holmes, "more of a keenness of distress at the crisis in which the Mother finds herself, though I have collected the feeling that in ordinary times, the older woman is perhaps fond of our young nun, or at least cognizant that in her she possesses a colleague of rare intellect and ability, perhaps even a successor to her office in due time."

I tried to envision the charismatic and logical-minded Sister Claire being changed into the dour figure of a Mother Superior, and was not certain I liked the thought, yet said:

"Well, that makes me worry a tad less for she who brought us here."

"I think, Watson, that you have little need to worry where

Sister Claire is concerned, for she has repeatedly impressed me throughout this case. Her acumen has spoken for itself, and in several of her deductions she has been downright masterful."

I was glad to hear this, but my contentment fell when he added:

"Save in one particular, where she failed most miserably."

"Her negligence in reporting the sounds she heard in the night?" I hazarded to theorize.

"No, Watson, for in that she erred only via a species of caution which held a certain logic."

"Then in what way?"

"I refer to her lapse in perception."

I did not ask what this was, but waited.

"In the account she gave us at the hôtel, Watson, I think she was correct in identifying that three different parties had serially passed her door on those separate nights, but was wrong in missing a vital clue in her deductions as to the nature of the first party who was out in the impenetrable darkness, for by her description of the steps which awoke her on that first occasion, I can tell you, the clandestine intruder was not a woman, *but a man.*"

*****

"A man?" I all-but thundered, for the idea of some anonymous male wandering at liberty through a house of women in the night seemed an assault upon all propriety.

"Yes," Holmes clarified, "if you remember, at the hôtel I asked her a clarifying question concerning this visitation, even requesting she mimic the stride with her own feet, and the stride she described was that of a man, for what she took to be slowness was in truth the greater length of a clandestine male stride, even one hampered by the limp she noted. If I am correct, I think the heart of the crime lies close to understandable, and the rôle of the guilty all but revealed to me."

"Remarkable," I said. "And what of the account of the ghost in the undercroft three years ago"

"Unrelated," Holmes told me, dismissively.

I did not wish to let that rather curious incident go so easily, and asked:

"No connection at all?"

"Watson, I think you rather like the idea of a resident ghost," he said with a small smile.

"Well, it *was* interesting, one must admit," I said in my defense.

"Were a place as old as this not endowed with tales of ghostly trespass, it should be the only building in Europe not to be so adorned."

"All right, but how do you explain that episode of supernatural claims?"

"A fortnight's collective hysteria, without relation to our matter, though I've no doubt the stories of noises in the undercroft, rats, most probably, did serve to delightfully shatter the boredom that unavoidably dwells within a cloistered life, and such stories spread like a wildfire, growing more lurid with each telling, until had Mother not stepped in, it is probable the most fancifully-minded of the community here should have told of encountering the devil himself, and requested an exorcist from Rome."

Bringing talk back to the present, I allowed:

"It did surprise me to hear the Mother Superior, who strikes me as a sound-natured sort of person, admitting she had not searched the quarters of the sisters, because none could possibly have a venal motive."

'Naïve, perhaps, but she does, I think, know her companions well, and I concur with her that greed motivated none of that community to undertake the theft of this sacred object."

"Might greed perhaps not be the only possible motive?" I posited.

"There you are correct, Watson, for one may also think of revenge, malice, psychological incapacity, or a simple prank, for that matter, though I lay some of those motivations aside for the present as being unlikely, for the footfalls in the night are surely connected."

"Holmes, was it one of the sisters, do you think?"

"An 'inside job' as they say on the streets of London? I do mingle it into several theories I have formed, though certain facts I hope to attain will render the actions of the guilty much clearer."

He guided me to one of the two doors that led outside, a sort of secondary entrance, and spent the next minute examining it, both with the naked eye and the lens he removed from his pocket.

"It has not been forced," he announced, "or coerced to unbolt itself, nor would it yield easily to even a master's pick. I, myself, should require at least a minute to see my way through such a fine old lock as this. I tell you, Watson, in the Middle Ages men knew how to build lasting things."

He then pulled open the door, showing it to be noisy in the extreme, owing to its age, and under his touch the handle clacked and the hinges creaked so jarringly that I thought the sounds must surely carry across half the convent, a thing that had not been reported.

"I think it unlikely, don't you, Watson, that anyone could come in through this portal during the latest hours of night, without awakening half the resident population?"

"What about the main door, then?"

"It was barred from inside, a barrier even the most adept of burglars would find difficult to manage, preferring a window in that case, or even the rooftop as a means of entry."

"By process of elimination, is that what likely happened?"

"The layout here does not favour an un-admitted party," he said, "for as I observed at our approach, there are few windows that open, even in the bedchambers of the nuns, and the rooftop would lead to nowhere in particular, and is most steep. Thus there are but these two outer doors, amid several inside ones which serve only to lead from hallways to hallway, wing to wing, yet none of those allowing egress to the outer world. Oddly, Watson, I would dub this humble convent more secure than many a military fortress I have visited."

"But clearly a thief has entered through some means."

"Yes, Watson, that fact is strongly suggested, as is his masculine identity, but the question arises *when* did he enter?"

"It is more a question of when and not how?"

"How I think I know, that being with the aid of a sister who resides here."

Ah, an "inside job" indeed. This fact was somewhat shocking, for all that I was not sure it should have been.

"No," I was told, "the primary question is *when* did the thief make his entrance?"

"Isn't it invariably the way of thieves to come, as the saying has it, in the night?"

"Think back to the timing of the footfalls in the passageway, and our young friend's account of them at the hôtel, for in that lies a profound clue."

"So the thief arrived the night before last, when Sister Claire heard him?"

"No later, certainly, though I think much earlier still."

"Meaning he could have been here much longer? Concealed?"

"I think amid the everyday goings-on of this religious community, an intruder was here, his trespass hidden, aided by a member of the convent."

With those portentous words we came to the chapel, empty now in the middle hours of the sunny afternoon. It was a prepossessing church, as fine as those which lay in many larger towns across France, having been built centuries before in a time of ardent faith, when it seemed all the most worthy actions of man had God as their object. It contained several rounded arches of the Romanesque style, and on the wall behind the east-facing altar a mural had been painted, depicting Judgment Day, and angels receiving the Resurrected into the gardens of Heaven.

Holmes paused in the entryway off the inner hallway of the convent, and looked about him, but seemed less impressed by the mural than was I.

"Up there in the choir loft," he indicated, "is where I conjecture Sister Claire stood in the night when she espied one of the elders among her sisters affecting to return the cross to the altar."

"A most puzzling action," I said.

"Nay, Watson, it is the most telling fact of all."

"How so?"

"Does it not inform you of something vital? Or at least suggest it most strongly?"

I attempted to penetrate his meaning, and while few possibilities presented themselves under my contemplation, I finally allowed:

"Some member here had become aware that the cross had been taken, and put a stop to it, returning it to its place, perhaps after chastising the guilty and obtaining a promise that such a deed would not be repeated, only for it to occur once more soon after?"

"In the scenario you describe, why should the elder nun who learned of the theft and who sought to rectify it, not have stepped forward this morning and revealed to her superior the identity of the guilty party, thus putting things right once again?"

"That is the telling fact?"

"It is."

There I was again stumped, for why, indeed, should the nun who had been seen returning the cross to the altar not do just as Holmes had suggested? After a long moment I confessed my ignorance as to her motive.

"I think, Watson," he told me, "the answer there is that something prevented her from speaking out. I refer to the consequences of her breaking her silence."

"What consequences could those be, Holmes?"

"Fear, guilt, or love," he said plainly. "It will invariably be one of those."

"I see."

"I think it possible her silence weighs heavily on her soul, and is not of her choosing, but is perhaps a lesser evil in her eyes. But I ask, is it not telling that all sisters are accounted for, and none are missing? Think on that, Watson."

I did so as I watched him step away from me and go to the altar itself, which I saw was covered by a stark white cloth of fine weave, upon which lay a circular depression, caused by the cross resting there for a considerable time. Holmes peered at this and at the floor around this holiest of places, then as quickly as he had drawn near to all of this, he moved away.

"There is little to be told here," he informed me, "nor did I expect there to be, but the chapel layout itself tells a little more."

He pointed around us.

"Note, my good Watson, there is no outside door within the chapel proper, only the single entryway which opens not into the outer world, but into a hallway that runs through the convent, with the wings containing the sleeping cells of the sisterhood barely forty feet distant in either a north or south direction. This is a chapel built to serve a resident population, not the outer rank and file of mankind from the town."

"Then to enter and commit this unholy crime," I offered, "our guilty party passed though the convent itself, just as Sister Claire heard on those two nights."

"Indubitably so. This tells of either a supreme confidence on the part of our thief, or considerable audacity, for there is risk in moving among so many would-be witnesses."

"Yet the thief undertook his crime twice last night," I summed up, "if the object was seized from him by the unknown nun and returned, as I think you are saying was the case."

"Yet, Watson, for all this movement about, there was to our knowledge but one sister in all the place, beyond she who was in the chapel, who heard telltale movement that night."

"Sister Claire, yes, but she mentioned she is a light sleeper, and you yourself have noted her perspicacity and her powers of observation. Perhaps that is the explanation there for why no one else heard anything."

"Indeed, yet out of a dozen and a half women here, the majority in the north wing through which the trespasser was heard to move, not one detected this passing? Do you not think this odd?"

"I do, but fail to grasp..."

"The thief did not pass through the entirety of the convent, Watson, but almost certainly began the journey of ill-intent from *within* that wing itself, and from it the journey down to the chapel was much reduced, as was the resultant noise of his passing."

"So it *was* one of the sisters?" I asked, the idea unwelcome.

"Do you not grasp the testimony of our evidence, Watson? A male intruder was *harboured* in the north wing, in one of the small rooms there, for the duration of at least two nights, and likely more than this. A man has secretly been granted shelter here, behind the backs of the nuns who reside within this holy place, and has been given this by one of the senior religious, who took it upon herself to hide him, and doubtless feed him, and yet this nun moved to undo his first effort at crime when she returned the cross to the chapel's altar, only for him to steal it again."

"How do you deduce this?"

"It fits more facts than any other. The windows to the chapel do not, as you see, open. The doors to the outside were securely locked by Mother each night, with the main entrance barred by a section of Medieval oak that has kept all here safe for half a millennium. The noises were heard by one nun only, Sister Claire, whom, I think we will find resides in a cell close to the one illicitly occupied by he who should not have been here, a man who has a confederate among the sisters, unwilling though she may be, a nun whom this man has compromised in some fashion, so that she has sheltered him, and in the end failed to prevent him from stealing the cross, though she did attempt to do so."

"Then it is her tragedy, Holmes, that she was forced by some as yet un-grasped circumstance to fill this rôle, and it is doubtless to her present shame that the theft resulted from her grudging collaboration."

"Grudging, Watson? Perhaps."

Turning swiftly from me, Holmes said:

"Come, I have need to see the door to the crypts."

At his heels, my usual place, I went after him as he strode to a small and unobtrusive door at the northeast corner of the chapel, which led to the undercroft. We had just reached this place, and Holmes had paused before the lock, magnifying lens in hand, when a voice was heard from the doorway, calling our names.

*****

"Dr. Watson! Mr. Holmes!"

I turned toward the chapel's entryway and saw Sister Claire hurrying toward us, her face bearing a look of both relief and curiosity.

Holmes likewise rose and focused upon this approaching nun, who had brought us here from Paris.

"I am glad I caught you before you opened the crypt," Sister Claire called out.

"And why is that?" Holmes asked her.

"Why, so I can go in with you," Claire replied in a tone that said she'd thought the explanation self-evident: a tone which amused Holmes, as did so much about the woman, I had noted.

"But were you not to assist the Mother Superior in searching the cells occupied by the other sisters?" I asked.

"No, Doctor," she answered mischievously, "I explained to Mother that while anyone here might readily help with that task, I, perhaps, could be more useful in the company of you and Mr. Holmes."

I caught that she had been running to reach us, for there was a breathlessness to her words.

"Mother," she went on, "holds me to be a clever and insightful sort, you see, and trusts me, despite her pique at my... well, you know of my regrettable hesitation in reporting the noises I overheard on the previous nights."

"I dare say the Mother is wise in the first regard," Holmes

declared, "and shall forgive you in the second. You are welcome to be with me as I work, Sister."

The young nun smiled, pleased, and moved to my side, joining me in looking on as Holmes went back to what he had been about to do before her arrival. Though he had a key to the door, courtesy of Mother, he did not immediately employ it, but knelt just before the handle and lock, and examined these with utmost care. After a long moment of silence, he rose and pronounced:

"This lock has been picked by one with some small capacity for the undertaking."

"You can tell this due to striations on the brass plating, I suppose?" asked Sister Claire.

Holmes faced her with a look of approval and said:

"Precisely because of that factor."

Saying this, he fit the Mother Superior's key into the lock and with a great cracking sound it was turned and the bolt thrown back, then Holmes pushed open the door onto a stone staircase that went down into a condition of undisturbed blackness.

Air, cold as night, wafted up to touch the warmth of my face.

"Sister," Holmes said with a nod forward, "do humour me and look at the interior of the door and tell me what you see."

Clearly happy to accept this assignment, the nun advanced a trio of steps into the semi-darkness, then leaned low to gaze with intense focus before saying:

"Oh, my, there has been a captive kept here in the undercroft, or at least someone went in willingly but disliked his confinement enough to seek to break out again."

Looking benignly and with pride at the young woman, Holmes asked:

"That is true. And now enlighten me, if you please, as to

how this was deduced by you."

"I see signs on both the wood and the iron fittings around the handle that a large chunk of stone, doubtless taken from one of the tombs below, was used to batter against the door, as he who was housed in the crypt sought egress. Look, there are even bits of crumbled stone just below the doorway."

She dipped down and retrieved a segment of this to hold aloft for emphasis.

"Watson," cried Holmes, "I tell you this young person is splendidness itself! Sister, you are wholly correct, and I salute you, for you have seen what I hoped you might. Incidentally, someone with moderate competency in the act has picked this lock to gain entry, lacking Mother's key as I have used, and this person has indeed placed another within the space of the crypt, either with or without that party's initial approval, but this person has clearly sought release from this subterranean underworld, and employed brute force to no avail against the solidness of this great medieval door."

Holmes slapped a hand against the stout old oak to demonstrate its formidable nature as a barrier, though considering it was an entry down to a long-ago place of burial, my mind slipped out the question *a barrier against what?*

"Holmes, why was this hammering not heard?" I asked.

"An excellent question," my friend agreed. "I think a little test of the chapel's acoustics is in order."

Saying this he began to kick the door from the far side, then hammered several times, first with his fists, and then with the bit of stone which Sister Claire had found. I can testify that the noise was considerable, echoing off the chapel walls as it did, and doubtless had the capacity to carry far.

"Well that does raise the point of why these sounds were not heard and investigated," Holmes said once his experiment was through. "Firstly I think this was not a prolonged protest against the rear of the door, but possibly occurred just once, accompanying a time when whatever sister was bringing food to whoever was within."

"That must be why my treasonous sister agreed to relocate him to one of the empty cells in the north wing," said Sister Claire.

"And how did you know someone was harboured within one of the rooms?" Holmes asked her, for he had not shared his deduction.

Yet our companion explained easily enough:

"I have figured out that this person must have been lodged there for the latter part of his stay here, for otherwise, his movements would surely have been heard by more than just myself, whose room was, I now shudder to realize, close-by."

"Brilliance itself!" Holmes praised. "I had wondered what would motivate our unidentified nun to do this thing, as it was a far less secure situation to have this man she was aiding kept up among others of her order than down in the subterranean crypt, but the answer in short was his protests forced her to remove him from here and take him to the north wing."

Drawing a long breath Holmes said to Sister Claire:

"Owing to what we have deduced thus far, I think it safe to say the youngest among your number here can be ruled out as to guilt, leaving only the so-dubbed 'seniors' who could be a party to this perpetration, for it is they who would have the ability and authority to act little noticed in such a manner. Thus I must ask, whom is it among the order who can most readily be away from times when all or most of the others are gathered, for meals or some other collective activity?"

Claire gave this a moment's thought before answering:

"Three among the seniors come to mind. Sister John of the Cross, who manages our herb and vegetable gardens, Sister

Jeanne, the cellarer, and Sister Anais, who oversees our laundry."

"Then our pool of suspects narrows," Holmes declared, "and it is these whom I shall shortly question. Sister, had you to focus your suspicions on one in particular from among that trio, which would you select?"

Here Sister Claire halted and seemed ill at ease, before at last saying:

"Until this theft I should never have thought to suspect any of those whom I have named, nor any other sister here, young or old, but as suspicion seems to point to these three, I might, just perhaps, cite Sister John as one who bears particular attention."

"And why is that?" I asked.

"Because she is the most trusted of all here, save for Mother herself"

"Then that is a most dreadful possibility," I said, "for betrayal of trust is a horrid offense."

"I shall give her every benefit of doubt, I assure you," Holmes promised, "and only be led by the testimony of fact."

"But whomever could this man be," I asked, "for this Sister John of the Cross, or any nun here, to risk so much on his behalf?"

Here Holmes said nothing for a moment, nor did Sister Claire, though finally he replied:

"There we can only speculate, Watson, and speculation is not fitting. There are many rôles a man might occupy that could justify a woman in religious life risking much to aid him. Which of these possibilities it is, I cannot as of yet state."

Hearing this, a number of hypothetical connections rolled through my mind, until I asked:

"Holmes, might this man who was hidden herein still be below, in the undercroft?"

A strange frosty thrill passed through me at the thought that a foe might yet be in the subterranean crypts, waiting to spring forth at us.

"I think not," Holmes told me. "In fact I can nearly guarantee no one is currently down in the depths, but let us ourselves go below and see what clues might have been left behind in this clandestine act of a religious sister hosting an outsider below the very feet of her community."

Sister Claire hurried to retrieve candles from a table across the chapel, taking three in her hands and sticking several more into a pocket on her habit, before handing one each to Holmes and myself. Thus provided with light courtesy of my friend's ever-present tinderbox, we set off into the decidedly chilly crypt, where the cold air was redolent of time, dust, and earth.

Holmes went before us, his candle flickering as he advanced, I went last, and Sister Claire filled the space between us, which I thought might be safest for a woman.

"This is an ancient place, to be sure," I said, awed, as at last, after I'd counted sixty-two steps, we reached the stone floor.

I looked upward and saw rounded barrel arches of the roofing faintly illuminated above us, cobwebs dangling down from them like moss, their height at least two-dozen feet from the cold floor underfoot. It was not chilled enough to see my breath fogging before me in the orange radiance of the candlelight, but my skin went to gooseflesh all the same. The area around us was immense, larger by far than the church overhead, spreading as it did into spaces below the earth in all directions, stones fitted into the walls, and burials likewise fitted within the stones. Gazing about me I espied what surely must have been three-hundred tombs at least, under and upon the floor as well as in the walls, some elaborate, others modest, and all from times long ago.

Sister Claire spoke up, but her voice was tiny and quiet, as if the surroundings awed her to meekness, or the silence itself drank her words.

"From my studies of our convent's history I can tell you this undercroft incorporated much older crypts than those which were added when the foundations of the present church were laid in the eleventh century. There is no telling how venerable some of the tombs here are, but earlier than the time of Charlemagne."

Holmes seemed to lack the interest I found in hearing this, and was pushing onward into the darkness, his candle but a faint firefly-like glow a growing distance from where the Sister and I stayed closer together, as I found something in me was reluctant to lose all sight of the doorway behind and above us, its light a tiny rectangle now barely sufficient to dispel even the merest modicum of darkness.

"Ah," Holmes finally called out, "come and look upon this!"

Before I could advance protectively ahead of her, Sister Claire pressed past me in her eagerness to learn what the detective had found, and for far from the first time I found myself noting how buoyant were her spirits, and how keen her sense of fascination. It was small wonder she had so impressed her superior here in religious life, as she was now doing with the great consulting detective himself.

I reached Holmes a few seconds after the sister, and saw he was indicating a place beside a small stone tomb where a clean cotton sheet lay upon the ground, and a twisted blanket was tossed beside it.

Upon seeing this humble camp-site, Sister Claire noted:

"Those are of the variety we have upon our beds here in the convent!"

"Of course," agreed Holmes.

Resting on the plinth of another low tomb, that of—

Guillaume, Chevalier de la Aallée

Décédé en Anno Domini 1049

--were the remains of a number of candles, and also a plate, and a cup, and some chicken bones, along with a number of opened and empty tins, with a spoon left inside one.

"Someone has stayed down here for...." I saw the Sister's face concentrate and she finished, "for four days' time."

"How do you know it was four days?" Holmes asked her.

"I see this," she said, "because that empty tin there once held boiled beef, which was used in a soup served to us that day. It could not have been here before that time, because it was only delivered to our convent that same day by Monsieur Calvert, the town grocer, who has a contract to bring us certain supplies each week."

"Excellent!" Holmes cried, all but beaming pride, so impressed by this feat of reasoning was he. "I would further deduce that this stay ended two nights ago."

"Because that time-frame coincided with the noises I heard in the dark," Sister Claire stated, catching on at once.

"Yes," Holmes concurred, again pleased, "at which time I think whoever had been lodged down here was reluctantly transported up to an unoccupied room in the north wing for the duration of his time under the convent roof."

"Transported out of here because of the noise he made hammering at the door," I put in.

"I think the understanding between the man and his benefactress at that point," noted Holmes, "would have been that the intruding party would soon make his departure from the convent itself, though it may be he stretched his stay out into that second night, ending in the act of theft this morning."

"Then it was last night this person betrayed whichever of the elder sisters was harbouring him," Sister Claire surmised quite independently of Holmes, "by stealing the cross. She detected the theft before he could flee with the object, and replaced it upon the altar, as I saw from the choir loft, but this thief returned behind her back and completed the crime before making his way into the outer world. Thus one of my sisters who entered the chapel this morning at Lauds, though perhaps as startled as the rest of us to see the cross gone, knew more than her face revealed. Her culpability is more wounding than the fact of the crime itself, for all here are as family to me."

Here Sister Claire paused down in the crypt's darkness before despairingly adding:

"I am disheartened to think upon our chances of ever recovering the item, now that it is amid the corruption of the outer world. Someone will surely melt our relic for its gold, and pry loose its gems to sell off separately."

I considered this grim summation of the situation, and was about to speak words of hopefully more than hollow consolation, when from above and behind us came a terrible sound, as the door to the church, the one means of departing from the undercroft, closed with a jarring bang.

I whipped about so rapidly my candle flame was extinguished, and saw the stone staircase, which had been the only portion of the crypt to be even faintly illuminated by outside light, now rested in total darkness. Panic bloomed within me.

"Mr. Holmes!" Sister Claire exclaimed, and at the heels of the detective, who was already in motion, she hurried back up the stairs, her candle flame, as Holmes' before her, going out in the rush of their flight, making a dense darkness fill every corner of our surroundings until I re-lit my own flame.

I walked as swiftly as I dared across the floor to the stairs, my heart filled with worry until I came upon Holmes quietly scoffing to Sister Claire at the idea that someone would judge him so devoid of resources and talent as to be left imprisoned by the mere shutting and bolting of a door.

"Imagine," he laughed, no trace of trepidation in his tone, "thinking I should be vexed by so minor an impediment. What does our adversary take me for?"

"We have an adversary?" I asked. "I had thought the malign party here departed, and she who had aided him more a victim of some persuasion on his part."

"It seems she now makes herself something more than a thief's hapless dupe," said Holmes. "But give me a moment and I shall have us out of our predicament."

No idle boast, Holmes required but a matter of seconds to have the lock picked, but when he went to push open the door, it moved but fractions of an inch before him.

"Our unseen foe has placed some heavy object," he said with a grunt, "perhaps one of the wrought-iron candelabras from the wall sconces, before the door, creating a simple but annoyingly effective barrier."

"One of my own sisters has done this?" Claire said, disgusted.

"Do not despair," Holmes told her, "she has stalled me but a further moment. Tell me, Sister, have you knowledge of the technique used to upend a barrier wedged in position on the opposite side of a doorway?"

"I have not," the nun confessed.

"Then come close and observe," Holmes coaxed her, "it is quite an interesting demonstration of how the properties of physics can be applied against themselves."

While I cannot precisely explain how it was done, for my place in the back was blocked by two witnesses in the foreground ahead of me, I did see Holmes undertake a series of manipulations of the handle while drawing the door back toward its frame, and after he had repeated this several times, with both subtle and overt movements, I heard the metal pole that had been securing the door slip away and fall with a rattle to the chapel floor.

"Simplicity itself," he said to Sister Claire. "You see how in principle it is a reliable means of escaping what one's foe judged a foil."

Having said this, Holmes stepped back and with a gentlemanly sweep of invitation to his arm, allowed first Sister Claire and then myself to exit the undercroft before him.

"Who was it?" Sister Claire asked, as we came to be together in the slanted late afternoon sunlight within the fine Romanesque chapel.

"For a little longer that is a mystery," Holmes told her, "though by her action another clue was provided to me, and my focus narrows once more, so that I think within the hour I shall know every answer."

"What will you do next?" I asked.

"Sister," Holmes said, his gray eyes twinkling with merriment, "do explain my next course to my friend, will you?"

"I think, Doctor, that before Mr. Holmes shall ask Mother to gather a certain group of our senior-most sisters, there is another location he wishes to see."

"And," Holmes asked her, "which location have I in mind to investigate ere we go to the office of the Mother?"

"You will go to the north wing and locate which cell it was that harboured the man, and see what evidence he may have left behind there."

"Certainly, Sister," Holmes agreed with a laugh. "I ask you to take us to whichever of these unassigned rooms you think should be our starting point. Rely entirely upon your instincts."

With a polite gesture, Holmes bade Sister Clair to lead us, while he and I followed.

As I trailed my companions, my mind engaged in its ruminations, I was struck by the quite unanticipated thought that had he a daughter, doubtless Sherlock Holmes would have hoped that many of the qualities he was discovering within Sister Claire were resident in her.

It was a strange and unprecedented bit of contemplation, but one which somehow pleased me, showing an altogether human aspect within my cool-natured friend.

*****

The small, Spartan bedchamber to which Sister Claire instinctively guided us before any others would prove to be the correct choice for Holmes to investigate, and entering alone, lens in hand, he peered closely at the bed, before casting an--

"A-ha!"

--into the air, and with a pair of tweezers in hand, he lifted a single hair from the thin wool-stuffed pillow there.

Holding this strand before us, he announced:

"I have here a physical connection with our trespasser."

He motioned then for the sister and myself to draw closer, and held the strand up to the fading light of the window, late afternoon now unfolding outside, and I saw the single hair was black and had a slight curl to it, and as he placed it within a tiny glass vial which he set back within his pocket, Holmes told us:

"I think this hair might prove useful, for it suggests something most strongly."

"The hair colour of the probable thief, yes," I agreed.

Looking at me with a demi-frown of his high-set brow, Holmes said:

"And something more, I think, my dear Watson."

"Doctor," Sister Claire said, something close to patience in her voice, "I think one of the main suspicions here is that whichever among my sisters is aiding this man is doing so for a connection she deems more binding than even the vows she has taken to live within this holy life. There is the chance she is being coerced in some manner, yes, but given that she had the man safely shut within the crypt for several days, yet did not then reveal his presence to Mother or the police, a suggestion may be deduced that her cooperation was willingly given, whatever her larger feelings. Thus I think the most likely conclusion--and do correct me if I err here, Mr. Holmes--is that my as yet unidentified sister—"

I interrupted, for I grasped at last what my companions had before me, and the idea was a shocking one:

"That this sister possesses a tie in blood with this person!"

"Consanguinity," Holmes added, "does bind most strongly."

"Yes," I said, "there is undeniable truth there. So the value of the hair is not only that it may serve to identify the thief, once he is apprehended, but to suggest some familial similarity between this hair and the hair of one of the nuns."

"That is correct, Watson," Holmes granted. "While curly black hair is no rare thing, it is not possessed by majority of the local population. Thus it sharpens the odds that she whom we seek may have hair of a matching nature."

"Who among the three senior nuns you had in mind has hair that is dark and curly?" I asked our young companion.

"Two of the three I named," she answered. "Sister John of the Cross, who oversees our herbal gardens and who has, rightly or not, been the one I have thought most likely to prove our wrongdoer, and Sister Jeanne, our long-time cellarer."

"The cellarer being she who is in charge of supplies of

foodstuffs?" I asked.

"Yes," I was told.

"This clue may aid us little," Holmes admitted, "or it may aid us much, but now let us take ourselves back to the office of the Mother Superior, so that she might have these three seniors among her subordinates brought down, as I would now put some questions to them."

Ah, I reflected, *the end-game drew near....*

*****

In the office of the Mother Superior, who met us with a worried look almost concealed behind a fine outward control of her emotions, Holmes shared the course of the deductions which had arisen amid his work, and also the fact that someone had attempted to shut the three of us below ground, in the crypt.

"We would, of course, have found you there soon enough," said Mother, aghast at this revelation, "but the idea that someone within these walls conducted herself thusly shames me deeply."

"It was of little matter," Holmes assured her, "for it was the merest setback and all was soon made well once again. It was a desperate measure, and rather meaningless, telling me the party who acted in this manner stands frightened, and now operates from an impulse of something approaching raw panic."

"And you have narrowed the possibility of culpability down to three?" Mother asked.

"I believe I have, Madam," Holmes replied. "And I think it almost a certainty that one of the three has, for reasons not entirely annotated by the evidence thus far, sheltered within these consecrated walls he who has taken your treasure."

"Who are those among the seniors you wish me to have brought to you?" Mother asked with a certain regret, for she understood that one of these whom she most trusted was likely to be revealed a traitor.

"Those to whom I must speak are named to me as one Sister Anais, one Sister John of the Cross, and a third, Sister Jeanne."

I saw the weight of heartbreak descend onto the Mother Superior, for the women named were her contemporaries, having entered the convent in the same era in which she herself had taken her vows, and she doubtless regarded each as a lifelong companion.

"Well then," Mother said at last, aware of the ramifications of the course of action to which she was committing herself, "Sister Claire, do go forth and summon Sisters Jeanne, Anais, and John of the Cross to assemble here."

The young nun bowed her head and turned to see to this, and when she was gone, Mother said:

"I had hoped that the evidence should somehow point elsewhere, Mr. Sherlock Holmes, for this betrayal cuts at my very heart."

Turning a sympathetic gaze onto the woman, Holmes said:

"I bid you take comfort, Mother, in the fact that it may be the cooperation your sister has given this criminal was not given entirely of her free will, and if it was, even then I think she may have acted only because she faced a monumental sense of conflict within her."

"There would be some small ease should this be true," Mother Superior replied, "thus I shall reserve my fullest feeling until all is known."

So saying, the woman leaned forward at her venerable desk, and entered into a state of wordless prayer, leaving Holmes and myself--indeed leaving this very world, I felt--while we waited for those summoned to appear.

It was nearly ten minutes before this gathering came to

pass, with the return of young Sister Claire, and the assembling of three nuns, each somewhere between forty and fifty-five, I would have guessed. One was slightly taller than the others, one bore a wart on her nose, and the third had hands much afflicted with those markings dubbed liver spots. On none did I note any indications of open villainy, for all seemed prime examples of duty within their stations. Their faces, however, spoke of many emotions forcibly contained behind that much-practiced screen of sober calm which religious life demanded, though I did not have to possess Holmes' insights to also discern curiosity, tension, and a universal sense of nervousness, all of which were to be expected.

"Mother," said Sister Claire, again with a slight bowing of her head toward her superior, an indication that her task had been done, and an unspoken question as to whether she was to remain.

In answer to this, the senior-most among the nuns said:

"As you have been part of all efforts to bring closure to this crisis, you may remain in the background, Sister Claire."

"I thank you, Mother," the young woman answered.

Here the Mother rose and I thought despite her age and size she suddenly loomed tall, reminding me of a regimental colonel about to address a group of officers.

"My sisters," she began, "as you know I have asked that this English gentleman of some monumental reputation as a solver of mysteries, Mr. Sherlock Holmes, come among us here today in order that he might possibly bring enlightenment, and just perhaps recover that which is dear to us all, as it was to our departed sisters before us, and God willing, will be to those of our order yet to come in this temporal abode of the Church Militant."

One of the three sisters, the one whose name was Anais, said:

"I pray God this will be so."

As she had spoken, Holmes had looked at her with a concentrated, expressionless gaze, noting, doubtless as I, too, saw with a doctor's eye, the deep lines about her mouth, and the fact she seemed to slightly favour one leg over the other. He then inquired:

"Sister Anais, I detect signs that you do pull your stride ever so slightly to the left."

There was no question in his words, but the woman confirmed:

"That is so, sir."

"It is, I think, an affliction concerning the knee?" I spoke up to ask.

"Arthritis," Sister Anais answered. "I bear it without complaint, but God knows it seems to trouble me more with each passing season."

I thought of Sister Claire's description of the odd pace with which one of those she'd heard in the night progressed down the hall, and my excitement increased, as I wondered, given her limp, was this Sister Anais the one?

Though he offered no words of sympathy for the sister's admission of ever-worsening discomfort, Holmes turned to the Mother and ended my speculation by commenting:

"I thank you for bringing Sister Anais here tonight. I need detain her no longer."

"So quickly?" Mother asked.

"The effects of her affliction would not match the footsteps that were testified to by our witness. Sister Anais played no part in these events."

And it had seemed such a certain match, I thought.

Mother Superior heard Holmes' words, nodded, and instructed:

"Thank you, Sister Anais, you may return to your room."

The nun stood still for another few seconds, almost as if she were in a state of disbelief that her portion in this matter had truly ended so quickly, then with an obedient bow of her head she walked from the office and back into the hall, where I heard her footsteps receding down the passage, the sound uneven.

And so we were left with two, Sister Jeanne, and Sister John of the Cross. Each of these were senior nuns, and each held a position of some authority and responsibility, cellarer, and gardener, neither task easily earned, I felt sure, meaning each of the women had shown herself reliable under the judgment of her peers, yet one of these was likely to have been guilty of much wrongdoing.

"Mother," Holmes said quietly," may it be possible that I see the hair of these sisters?"

Somehow the request struck me as being much more than was readily implied, for I knew a nun did not display her head in a bare state. Thus it was a moment before Mother nodded her consent, and told her sisters:

"Pull back your wimples so that Mr. Holmes might view your hair."

The two stood still, as if dismayed by the request, and it was Sister John of the Cross who complied an instant before her sister, tugging back her head-covering far enough to show wavy hair, once black, now mingled with gray overcoming the darker strands. Like the hair of all nuns, it was cropped quite short to the scalp.

Holmes looked toward her and offered his thanks, allowing her to again cover herself.

With considerably more reluctance, but with obedience to her superior in the end, Sister Jeanne did the same, revealing that her closely-cut hair was curlier and dark still.

A familial match for what was found? I wondered, telling myself that even if it was, it could have been a matter of coincidence, and did not indicate undeniable guilt.

I had no sooner thought this than I saw Holmes step closer to this nun, and his eyes went up and down her form, covered as it was by a habit so bag-like I imagined it could reveal little to even his practiced gaze. Still, Holmes said:

"I see you have recently bruised the side of your left hand, sister. How was this injury acquired?"

"It was caused by a box in the cellar," she answered.

"What sort of box?" Holmes asked.

"Peaches, canned last harvest. They were inside a wooden crate."

"We have had crates of peaches taken from storage lately," Mother stated from behind her desk.

She truly wants neither of these to be guilty, I thought, taking note of this.

"And how did this cause a bruise?" Holmes pushed on.

"The crate slipped," Sister Jeanne said at once, "and trapped my hand between a table and itself."

"An object fell *upon* it?" Holmes pressed, looking harder now at the bruise, making the nun self-consciously pull back her hand under his stare of evaluation, and set it to her side.

"Yes," she insisted.

"Sister Jeanne, are you certain that bruise was not incurred by you striking something with your hand, rather than something striking it? For I tell you, to the trained eye there is a difference in what is left behind."

"I meant to say this," Sister Jeanne said, awkwardness now coming upon her, "I struck my hand itself against the crate's side."

"No, you didn't," Holmes said, his voice now lower, not threatening, but also without patience. "I know something on the subject of bruises and recognize that this this injury was caused neither by a crate falling onto it, nor, despite the trap of my suggestion, you striking an object. Come, Sister, will you not be truthful with me?"

"I tell you, sir, it was when the crate fell downward and--"

"No, no," Holmes interrupted, almost with regret. "Then it seems you leave the revelation to pass onto me."

I think those of us in the office who were neither Sherlock Holmes nor this Sister Jeanne subconsciously leaned forward at that instant, moving as one.

"Your injury," the detective stated, "was caused by someone squeezing your hand most tightly. Doubtless painfully so."

There was a pause amid the silence which came after this statement, and then Holmes asked:

"Sister Jeanne, who was it who forced this vice-like grasp onto you?"

The nun's face tightened, her eyes fearful.

"You have the wrong of things," she proclaimed, her voice misery itself,

"Madam, I would stake a year's wages that I do not."

"Sir, I tell you---"

"So I see even here you protect this person, as you shielded him these past days and nights, as you tried to protect him this afternoon, when you closed the door to the undercroft, thinking to trap me and my companions within."

There was a wildness in Sister Jeanne's eyes as Holmes said this, and I saw guilt spelled out there.

Before there could be any reply, though, Holmes turned to

the Mother and said:

"Standing as she does beside Sister Jeanne, Sister John of the Cross likewise shows me several interesting facts upon her person, such as her mania for nail-biting, and a fondness for candies obtained from the village and doubtless concealed away somewhere in her quarters, but none of what I see concerning her stands as germane to that which has brought me here. I think it is permissible that she be sent on, for upon the person of Sister Jeanne, I discern a number of interesting clues, this bruise so tellingly inflicted upon her by another being only one among them. I also see she has been starving herself these last days, so that she might pass her food along to another."

"It is true I had thought to myself that you have been looking gaunt all week," Mother said to the nun.

Holmes sighed at these tidings and said to Sister Jeanne:

"The fact, Sister, that you are cellarer and have access to foodstuffs, yet have utilized your own to feed another tells me much of your nature, and its innermost honesty, for you chose to go hungry rather than steal nourishment from the convent which has entrusted you. I am convinced you are a good soul who has been placed in a position that went beyond your capacity to put right, and thus you sought to achieve the best outcome for all, at a cost to yourself, as your injury shows. As I have judged you less than a villain, will you not follow through on that goodness I see within you, and make a full confession?"

The attention of the other three nuns fell fully onto Sister Jeanne, and my own eyes were riveted there as well, but though she opened her mouth to speak, still a hesitation ruled her.

"Sister," said Holmes, again almost with gentleness, "will you not confide the truth, lest I am forced once more to speak it for you?"

"You know the truth, sir?" Sister Jeanne asked, her voice wavering, filled with the agony of mortification, and even in the late-afternoon shadows of the office, I saw her face flamed with colour, her shame manifesting there.

"I do not know all things, no," Holmes said, opting for honesty over a bluff, "but I know much and theorize still more, and do hope you dispel what little ignorance remains on my part. Tell me who the man was, for though I have narrowed it to two possibilities, I can go no farther on the evidence I have gathered."

Sister Jeanne's head sagged and her eyes went to the floor, and though her mouth opened, no words came forth, though I think she did try to speak.

To my surprise, it was Mother Superior who broke the silence by asking in a tone that held both authority and compassion:

"Sister, was it *Jean-Claude* who came here, and brought this evil to us?"

At this Sister Jeanne's bowed head nodded but once, though it was enough, for upon seeing this Mother sank back into her chair, and I watched as her own face was overcome by an inrush of emotions. Still, it was with sympathy in her voice that she said something that quite mystified me:

"Oh, my beloved sister, my poor Jeanne...."

I was now puzzled, yet Holmes registered comprehension, as if one of the two possibilities he mentioned had fallen away, leaving only truth, and as for Mother, when she spoke again, it was to say:

"Sister Claire, Sister John of the Cross, you may leave us."

Though Sister John's face showed nothing as she left, Sister Claire gazed back toward Holmes and me, and also at Sister Jeanne, who stood on the floor, her body all but contracted in shame, and somehow I felt that like Holmes, the young nun understood all that I did not.

When she and her elder had gone and the door was shut,

Holmes said to we who remained:

"I had from the beginning held that a blood connection was hinted at behind the facts here, and thought perhaps the man was a brother come to these grounds for aid in a time of emergency, but now I find the truth is one that lays an even stronger claim upon the loyalties of the heart."

"Jean-Claude is my son," Sister Jeanne said hollowly. "My son, twenty years in age, born to me shortly after I came into the convent, his father a boy from town. It was my most terrible sin, and nearly my falling."

"Sister," Mother said, stepping around the desk and reaching down to take the other woman's hand, the one that was not bruised. "That sin has been forgiven through Christ, and in all the years you have remained since, it has never been repeated. Your devotion to holy life has been absolute, and as God has forgiven you, I and those few of us of a certain age who knew of this violation of your sacred vows forgave you as well, and have kept your secret. Sister, as you failed to come to me in the course of Jean-Claude's appearance here, do so now and confide all concerning your travails of these last days, for I see you have suffered much."

"It was not that I did not wish to come to you, Mother," the nun said, misery in her every word, "it is that I was prevented, not only for the love I discovered I could not help but feel for he who is my son, but because of the love I have for all of my sisters here."

"What...?" Mother asked.

"This Jean-Claude made threats against you all," said Holmes, intuiting Sister Jeanne's meaning.

The nun nodded and said:

"He swore if I revealed he was here, he would kill us all."

Anger swelled in me, and I asked:

"But why did he come here at all?"

"I discovered my son was a convict," she explained, "escaped from a prison farm where he had been sent to labour under the terms of his sentence for robbing and assaulting the owner of the forge where he was apprenticed at age fourteen. Eleven years he was given when he committed his crime at age sixteen, and was four years into this incarceration. He was a ruthless young man, but his conduct within prison was docile enough, so that as he explained to me, he was paroled off to a work-farm, and there he bided his time until he had a chance to break loose and flee."

"Which was likely his goal all along," Holmes told her.

She drew a deep breath and said:

"And after eluding pursuit for a week, in his desperation, his opportunities for concealment fading, he came to me."

"Why did he come here?" Mother asked.

"In the orphanage where he had been raised, I, of course, choosing to continue the religious life of my vows over bringing up my own child," her voice cracked as she said this, and I saw that choice long ago had been one of agony, "he, being clever and fearless, had found the records that named me as she who had given birth to him, and always remembering this, he had come seeking me here. He found me in the cellar, and though his appearance frightened me, he being dirty and wild about his eyes, clad in mismatching clothing he had stolen along the way, I knew without an instant's pause that it was my secret son, at once my shame and my beloved, who stood there before me."

I tried to imagine such a moment, all that would have composed it, the terror, the joy, the fear, and I truly felt for this Sister Jeanne.

"What did he say to you," asked Mother, and I noted Holmes, though listening attentively, had not broken his silence for more than a minute.

"It was not a reunion touched by happiness, for he was like a hunted animal, and said that if he were caught, he would be most savagely beaten, and rather than return to work on the prison farm, would be thrown into the deepest dungeon in the county, his sentence extended to twenty years, a thing he said he could not bear. 'Help me, Mother,' he cried out, 'for you have never helped me before, nor have I ever asked you for anything until this.'"

How, I thought, *could any woman have been expected to deny her child at such a time?*

"Oh, Jeanne," said Mother Superior, "my heart does move for the choices you were forced to make, both long ago and in the here and now."

"I confess," Sister Jeanne told us, "I gave him candles and hid him in the undercroft those first nights, and took him my own food rather than steal from the stores entrusted to me, but he claimed he could not bear it down there, that the walls closed in on him, too much like a prison cell. When I visited him on the fourth day, he hammered on the door at my approach and I told him I could hide him nowhere else, and that is when he suddenly changed, becoming most violent, frightening me, grabbing my hand and crushing it with bruising force, and telling me he would kill all of my sisters if I did not move him elsewhere. Thus I did so, though it was a perilous thing for him to stay so close to where so many lived, and I told him at last that he must not seek to stay long."

"Fortunate then for all residing here," I said, "that it was but one among you here who heard his movement, for I think had others looked out in the night, so desperate a man as a prisoner may have sought to stop their witnessing against him."

At this Holmes at last broke his silence saying:

"Yes, for after time in the feral confines of a prison, a man's instincts become oriented to violence as means of self-preservation. It was good judgment on the part of Sister Claire that she did not step out into the hallway to investigate those sounds she heard."

"She is a young woman of wisdom," agreed Mother.

"I take it this young man was no more content in the room than he had been in the undercroft?" Holmes asked.

"No, sir," Sister Jeanne confirmed. "And the matter deteriorated, as this man...my son...though he claimed he was desperate to be away once the authorities had lessened their search for him, made comments last night that horrified me, speaking as he did of the physical appearance of several of the younger nuns he had seen here, Sister Claire chief among these."

My anger now was stoked at this revelation, and I thought I could have cheerfully throttled this beastly young man.

"At that point I told him he must go or I should expose his presence here. He rushed at me there in the little room, and put to my throat a knife stolen from the kitchen, and swore he would kill many of us before he would be re-taken. I trembled, believing him, and I was at a loss for words, when he said, 'So you want me to go peacefully? I think I could get good coin for that cross in the chapel. Enough to fund my flight far from here.'"

"And you reaction?" Mother asked.

"I did not want him to do that, but I knew the virtue of my sisters, and of course our very lives, were far more important, so I admit there in the darkness, his knife to my throat, I said yes, take the cross and be gone, and do not come back here, Jean-Claude."

"A difficult choice," I said.

"He then left me then to do so, yet overcome by guilt I went with him, the other instance of walking in the hallway which Sister Claire heard, and went to the chapel, watching as he did that loathsome crime of stealing the cross from the altar. Yet I felt an outrage rise even above my fear, and as he was moving to depart from this holy place, I came after him and prayed that God would give me words to change his heart. And so when I came to him I told him of my feelings for him as a babe, how I saw him but once before he was placed in the orphanage, and while he grew angrier for a moment, saying I rejected him in exchange for religious life, I felt finally a small miracle happen, as his soul softened, and I held him to me there in the darkness of the hallway before the outer doors, both of us weeping, and I thought of all I could have had in raising my child, and the pain of the choice I made to remain a nun was as nothing I had known in all my life."

She wiped tears from her cheek and said:

"He gave me the cross and said put it back on the altar, he would simply go, and vowed then that he would do all that he could to never again fall into the sin of criminality, but would remember the example of his mother, and learn better ways. I rejoiced at hearing him make this promise, and saw a change had come upon him even as I watched him slip out into the night, praying as he did that all would be well with him and that his declaration to become an honest man would last."

"Then you went back to the chapel and replaced the cross, as Sister Claire saw you do," Holmes told her.

"She witnessed this?" Sister Jeanne asked in amazement.

"She was in the cloisters above the choir gallery, Holmes revealed, "though she did not grasp your identity."

"Oh, I did not know," Sister Jeanne said, subtly awed to learn this.

"And yet," said Mother, "even though you say this transpired, and I do believe you, the fact remains the cross was gone before dawn."

"Yes," Sister Jeanne agreed, her voice almost a moan of despair, "my Jean-Claude must have lost that moment of grace we found together, and come back for it."

"Clearly," Mother agreed. "And now he could be twenty miles from here."

"No," Sherlock Holmes entered the narrative to state, "wherever this straying child may be now, near or far, I think he did not return for the cross."

"It was not him....?" Sister Jeanne said, marveling, as if clutching at a ray of hope.

"Then you suspect someone from within the convent, Holmes?" I voiced. "Another of the nuns?"

"Hardly, Watson," he replied, "but rather I give voice to a suspicion I have harboured for some time as I have investigated here, and to confirm it, I beg you, Mother, ask Sister Claire to re-join us, if you would."

The Mother Superior tugged a cord on her wall, and a novice of still-tender years, wearing large eyeglasses, came to the door.

"Do bring Sister Claire to me," Mother instructed.

When the sister had gone to accomplish this, Mother said to Holmes:

"Can you tell me of your suspicion?"

"A moment, if you please," he said, "for there is a question I would first pose to our young friend."

Several minutes passed amid relative silence within the Mother's office, until a small tap sounded outside her door, and Sister Claire was admitted, as Holmes had asked.

"Mother?" the young nun inquired, her pose meek, all the bounteous energies I had often seen in her held quietly within.

"Mr. Holmes has need to speak with you, Sister," said the Mother.

Turning toward Holmes, her face marked by a placid fondness I think she had come to feel for the detective, as I think he held a respectful regard for her, Holmes said:

"You have spoken of hearing footfalls beyond your door on

three occasions in two nights. This is correct?"

"It is," Sister Claire concurred.

"Ah, and yet from the account of Sister Jeanne here, I mark but two occasions when she could account for the authorship of such sounds. Thus, the story of the unknown footsteps in the night does serve to reveal all."

With a jolt I realized this was so, and understood I had been so focused upon the nun's narrative and the shocking nature of what her blood-son had carried out, that the ramifications of this fact had slipped past me.

"The third footsteps...the unrecognized ones I was unable to identify," Sister Claire said, awe and horror battling within her expression.

"Holmes," I said, "there was an unaccounted presence within the convent!"

"Quite so, Watson," my friend agreed.

"Then that means..." Sister Claire began, her keen mind racing to pull together the pieces into one. Grasping the truth, she gasped and said, "There was a second man in hiding!"

"Correct," began Holmes. "As I have suspected, these holy environs have, unknown even to this Jean-Claude, played host to a second individual, whose identity I suspect is none other than a fellow convict from the labour-farm, who followed his fellow criminal's example and made his escape. In secret he doubtless trailed Jean-Claude and in time followed him here, entering the convent with subterfuge, being perhaps well-practiced as a burglar, thereafter lurking in shadows, skulking through the darkness, watching but remaining unseen and sheltered herein. When he witnessed the theft of the cross and its return, he grasped the price it would bring if he sold it to a fence somewhere along his flight, I think it was this subsequent intruder who affected the second theft, and fled with it into the darkness."

"Then it truly is lost!" Mother said with sadness.

"And the fault is mine, Benoîte, all mine own!" Sister Jeanne said, addressing Mother by her oldest name as she pressed her face into her hands, weeping with drear.

"No," Holmes said, "do calm yourself, Sister, for there is a hope that I may yet retrieve that venerable cross."

Turning from the Mother to Sister Claire, he demanded:

"The noise you described to me back at the hôtel, the one I asked you to demonstrate, and which you did with such commendable accuracy, was of a right leg being dragged in a limp. Had it been the left leg revealed by your testimony I might have erroneously focused upon Sister Anais, but her affliction is of the opposite limb. The man who has hidden himself here, watching from the corners and moving in the darkness, not always heard by you, Sister Claire, for I think he went far and near inside this place, moves with a decided limp in his right leg, and thus he is unable to travel quickly, nor likely is he willing to go far without pain overcoming him. Thus I think it possible he yet remains at some little distance, within my reach."

"God be praised!" the Mother Superior breathed.

With a vivid intensity that was almost savage, a predatory light came into Holmes' gray eyes, as he told us:

"When hiding in a rural setting such as this, a man's thoughts go toward isolation, just as in a city he would seek the aid of friends. Hereabouts this means the forest will be his cover. Therefore I ask you to consider now, Sisters, the woods beyond these grounds to a distance of three miles, the more deserted and untraveled the better, and name any feature therein, natural or made by the hands of man, a cavern, a great hollow tree, anything which could shelter a desperate soul."

Almost at once Sister Claire said:

"The ruined oratory in the forest."

"Tell me of it!" Holmes ordered, all excitement now.

"It is a roofless stone structure," Claire began, "built many centuries ago, perhaps in the days of Charlemagne, who endowed so many houses of holiness hereabouts, and it was once used as a scene of private meditation by sisters of our order, who prayed there before they took their final vows. It is windowless and has no door, and is much overgrown, with weeds amid the bare floor and trees which press right to the walls themselves. No one visits there any longer, but anyone who goes into the woods could surely find it without much difficulty. It sits perhaps a half-mile away."

Without pause, Holmes hurled himself from his chair and into the hallway.

"I thank you, Mother," I said to our hostess as I rushed after my swift-moving friend, though I was soon startled to realize that a third party was traveling with me.

"Since I set this investigation into motion by seeking out Mr. Holmes," said Sister Claire, "I must see it through by going with you to the oratory."

"I don't think that is wise," I answered, "for if there is a convict hiding there, dangers will abound."

"I am unafraid," the little nun told me.

I was about to protest further, when from ahead of me, nearly at the great oaken doors which opened to the convent's grounds, Sherlock Holmes called:

"Let her come, Watson, as she can be our guide!"

And so I could speak no further prohibition against our young companion.

*****

The afternoon was at its last hold before surrendering to evening and we had set out so quickly that Holmes had not even paused to secure a lantern for later aid.

Moving with the swiftness of youth, more than keeping pace with Sherlock Holmes, Sister Claire stayed at his elbow and told him:

"You see where the woods begin, at the pasture's edge? If we drift southward a moment, we should see the pathway that goes into the forest proper, and from it the oratory is but two furlongs farther in."

Holmes was listening, but also casting his eyes to the ground as he led us toward the wilds, and at one point he froze mid-step and set an arm outward to likewise halt the sister beside him.

"Do peer downward!" he called, pleased, his voice rising a little high.

"A track!" Sister Claire declared, seeing it herself. "And look, the right footprint is blurred by dragging."

Her eyes are keen indeed, I thought, adding:

"Then it is surely our man!"

I also saw that though the open landscape was well-lighted in the radiance of the sun hanging low above the horizon, this was less so under the canopy of trees, their leaves broad and thick with the plentitude of summer, and I felt a chill as I considered how we were soon to enter into uncertain conditions amid shadows, where a dangerous man almost certainly waited.

With this in my thoughts, I said:

"Holmes, though we are doubtless indebted to Sister Claire for her insights and guidance, surely it is wisest she stay behind at this point, for think of the hazards ahead in this undertaking."

Without waiting for Holmes to render a verdict, the nun said:

"Let me continue on with you. I feel honor-bound to see all

made well, for I know my own rôle in allowing matters to proceed these last nights, leading to the theft of our dear cross. Please do not send me away, let me be among this party, for surely I can be useful in some manner."

"You must not indict yourself in the events of this week," Holmes told her, "for we now know what a house of cards all was, and violence may well have been the legacy of the two dangerous men who hid themselves under your very roof. The fact you stand here alive and well, as are all your sisters, says much regarding the wisdom of your conduct."

"I thank you," said Sister Claire, "but may I not--"

"You may continue with us, if that is your wish," Holmes answered, "for I do not command you."

At these words I saw gladness sweep over the young woman's face.

Thus into the woods we went, as my friend and I had so often in times past, when we had likewise sought enemies almost without number. As he moved at a cautious pace, Holmes pointed downward at random here and there, showing Sister Claire various indications of his quarry's passing, a broken twig on a sapling, a crushed growth of moss on a north-facing stone, signs I largely failed to catch with my own eyes, but which the perspicacious nun discerned with eagerness.

"These are hours old," Holmes informed her, "and yet I feel a drawing certainty that our man is not far ahead. Thus, quiet, now, I bid you both, if with stealth we are to spin our net about him today!"

We went on, moving more slowly now, but still with a steadiness, until at the farthest distance which I could perceive through the trees, some being thick and venerable, I spied the half-ruined stones of the oratory, and it was then Holmes raised a cautionary hand, and whispered:

"Here, Sister, I must bid you, do stay, for I know not what I might find rising in opposition to our approach. Watson, keep low."

Sister Claire did as he said, though I saw her thoughts were as focused upon the destination as my own, and as she stepped behind a tree-trunk and crouched, minimizing her figure, her habit already dark amid the shadows, I could discern only too strongly her desire to go onward with us. I sympathized, but knew Holmes' caution was for the best.

Weaving soundlessly beside me, the great consulting detective and I crept onward, making scarcely a sound, until we drew near the Medieval structure, its ancient stones rising a little above my own height, its roof long gone, though the place retained a rough majesty, haunted by the echoes of prayers once chanted within. It was a place of piety now perhaps occupied by an immoral felon, in rude violation of so holy a site.

With a last slinking motion, Holmes came to the structure and looked carefully within, only for me to do likewise an instant after, and release a gasp, declaring:

"Though empty of the man, look, Holmes, there is the cross itself, protruding above that makeshift knapsack!"

"It is indeed, my dear Watson," said Holmes peering inward at the small but beautiful artefact of an age of faith, its gold catching every ray of light that fell through the trees. "But have a care, for the robber who purloined that precious object was here but a moment ago."

"Did he flee at our approach?"

"It is not unlikely."

"Then doubtless he still lurks somewhere nearby!" I said uneasily.

Holmes gazed about him for the merest moment before his eyes fell onto something on the earth, then rising and with alarm he cried:

"There are the tracks which show his exit, and they lead.... Grab the item, Watson, but hurry, for we have left our young companion unguarded!"

This spoken, he flipped about and began to rush back the way we'd come, down fifty interposing yards of trees which blocked our sight for more than a few paces distance.

I entered the ruins of the old oratory and lifted the cross from where it rested, finding it heavier than I had expected, and warm under my fingers. With it in my hold I hurried on in the direction Holmes had gone, and had reached the last ten paces when I froze, as I saw my friend had as well, and like him I began to stare at a sight which sent horror radiating through my every cell, for there next to the tall tree where we'd left her five minutes before, was Sister Claire, her face calm but her eyes locking onto those of Holmes, while behind her stood a large, wild-faced man with hardened eyes and hair askew, who was holding a blade against the young nun's throat.

Though my French had improved with this stay in the Gallic country, it remained imperfect, but despite this I understood only too well the threat in the wild-man's next words, as he declared:

"Move any closer and I will open the girl's neck."

Holmes did as he was bidden and stay rooted to the ground, his eyes granting little insight into his thoughts, his expression neutral, almost placid, though I suspected below this outer calm his brain was whirling.

"As you say," he finally allowed, sounding meek, unchallenging, yet I knew that in the face of danger he was always alive with energy and intention.

"You are police?" the man growled, feral as a forest cat, his eyes bloodshot and bugging in their sockets.

"We are not," said Holmes.

"No? Then why did you come here seeking me?"

"We are aiding the sisters of the convent in the lawful return of that which you have taken from them," Holmes told him.

Was such utter candor the correct strategy? I wondered.

"A thief has a right to claim what he has gained by his efforts," the big Frenchman, tall as Holmes and broader at the shoulders, his physique like a wedge, tossed back disdainfully, and I saw he was missing a tooth at the fore of his wide mouth. Everything about him spoke of strength, and a capacity for violent action.

"So I have heard it stated by my adversaries," said Holmes, "though it is a maxim I have never, myself, embraced."

"Sir, you do not need to hold the blade so tightly," Sister Claire beseeched her abductor, almost at a whisper. "I cannot run from you, and you are hurting me without reason."

"Speak again and I will hurt you much worse," the criminal vowed, jerking his lower arm, the one holding her crushed against him, making the nun gasp, winded. "Little one, I can break your ribs like matchsticks, simple as anything."

"There is no need to injure her," I called, only for the man to glare back at me with vicious loathing, his eyes like those of a rabid wolf.

"He does not injure me, Doctor," Sister Claire risked breaking the mandate on her silence to say.

Ignoring her, the thief spoke again, commanding:

"If you have guns upon your persons, either of you, you will now place them on the ground, or you'll see her die."

Then moving the knife up from Sister Claire's throat to the side of her neck, above where the carotid artery rested, he barked:

"Do it with care, for if I see any efforts at trickery, I swear by the soul of my dead father, I will kill her."

"I have no gun, nor does my companion," Holmes told him.

"Is that so?" the man replied, and I saw his face brighten with evil delight. "Then you are fools to have come into the forest, chasing after me without weapons. Take off your jackets, then, and let me verify you speak the truth."

I followed Holmes' example and shed my coat, as he did his great Ulster, which with gentleness, as if it were a friend, he laid upon the earth.

"You see I speak the truth, we carry no firearms," Holmes said.

"A gentleman would not take such things into a church," I added.

The criminal then laughed a deep, hard chuckle, and said:

"So you hold yourselves gentlemen, do you?"

"Oh, yes," Holmes answered, "and never lose sight of that fact, however lacking notions such as honour may be in you."

"Are all Englishmen such fools as the pair of you, who chase a beast to his lair without a spear? You do make this too easy for me."

"Let me propose an end to this," I said. "Tie the three of us to trees and be on then, for you have clearly won this hour."

In reply the Frenchman regarded me as if I was the most profound of imbeciles, and marveled a moment before saying:

"I am afraid you will not be so fortunate today."

I thought then:

He means to kill us all!

"She is a woman, and little threat to you," Holmes said, and here he stepped a cautious trio of paces forward, closing the distance toward he to whom he spoke, "If you have violent business with the two of us, man to man, then be that as it will, but do you wish your legacy stained by the slaying of a nun?"

"Let her go," I added. "You can be long gone into the night by the time she alerts others."

I saw the man consider this, his eyes, one of them bruised as if he had recently been struck, moving from one of us to the next.

"I do not think that idea appeals to me," he said. His smile was gleeful when he added, "I noticed this one on those dark nights I hid inside her convent, and think I might just take her with me, when you two are dead."

"I know you have never been convicted of murder," Holmes said, risking yet another step, but still a dozen paces distant, "or you should not have been paroled to the prison-farm, so do not add to your crimes the one which will send you to the guillotine."

The man laughed louder now and said:

"When I woke this morning that was still true, but no longer."

"So this morning you made an end to the man who unknowingly led you to the convent," Holmes said, comprehending the criminal's meaning. "Well as they say, there is scant loyalty among thieves."

The tragedy! I thought, hearing that Sister Jeanne's son, Jean-Claude, was dead, so soon after his mother's tears had inspired him to redemption.

"He betrayed me first!" the man roared, "and struck me in the face, as you see by my bruised eye. It was he who leapt onto me, the little fool!"

"No doubt he did," Holmes told him, and he took two more steps now, "but I would wager the whole truth is that he sought to return the cross you stole."

Seeing that he had now crossed half the distance which had separated them, the Frenchman shouted out:

"Quit advancing, or this tiny nun here will pay for it!"

Holmes lifted his hands in supplication and paused where he stood, offering:

"As you direct. But tell me, how was it you encountered your fellow convict this morning out here in so unlikely a place?"

"It was he who first found this little stone church here before sunup, and I who came upon him, seeing in it a place of solace, as he had an hour before me. He saw that I had the cross in my hold, and rose and shouted angrily that I must turn it over to him, that he might return it. It was madness, and I told him so, as why should I surrender this object when by selling it I might secure enough money to see me across the nation, to a hiding place high in the Pyrenees?"

"And it was then, at your refusal, that he attacked you?" Holmes said, and there was an ersatz hint of sympathy in his voice, which the convict discerned and, however unlikely, seemed to latch onto with appreciation.

"You do understand how things were, then," he said, "he tried to take the gold cross from me, meaning to return it to the nuns, the fool. He came on, filled with fury, and threw many blows at me, but I am an old tomcat who has been in a score of brawls in the alleys of Paris, and he was really little match for me, being smaller and inexperienced, despite his youth, he twenty, I nearly twice that. Also I had my knife, and he had none, and so it was soon over, and the look on his face when my blade went through his conniving heart...ha! You can find him tossed into a thicket behind the ruined church, his body covered over with brambles, where the worms and mice can have him."

At that moment I thought of Sister Jeanne, destined to learn the tragic news that she had lost her child so soon after meeting him for the first time since he was a babe.

"So having killed once, you do not shrink from killing three more," Holmes said, and now he flashed a quick and almost involuntary smile. "Murder is a bargain crime, as they say, for no matter how many victims he accrues, a man can be punished for it but once."

"I ken to that," said the criminal, "and shall remember you by that wise saying. But now it is time to end your intrusion here, and since she now knows too much, I find with regret that I can no longer take this pretty little one with me as my hostage."

I saw a tightening of the arm which held the blade, and knew with horror that he was preparing to snuff out the life of the bright little nun. Yet I then witnessed something so brave and bold and unlikely it will always reside in some untarnished place in my brain, for as the murderer drew back the knife, Sister Claire reacted to save us all, stomping hard upon his foot, then driving her elbow into his mid-section before slipping away, fleet as a hare. Yet even there she was not finished, for as the big man reeled, cursing, she reached low and tore up a handful of sandy soil, and this she flung into his eyes, blinding him for a small moment.

It was the only opening Sherlock Holmes and I needed, as my friend exploded forward, covering the distance between himself and the man in several great leaping strides, I, too, ran at him, attempting to come up behind him in a flanking maneuver, opening a double front upon this enemy.

The Frenchman, however, was well-practiced as a fighter, and though he had a limp in one leg, and the other foot was doubtless aching from where Sister Claire had stomped upon it, he twisted quick as a rat terrier, his eyes still convulsively blinking and streaming tears of violation, and slashed toward me. But this was a ruse, for he shot about to stab at Holmes, whom he instinctively understood was his most formidable enemy, and this deadly strike missed only because Holmes was quicker still in drawing back.

In the tiny instant before the convict could pull the knife back toward himself, Holmes grabbed a broken tree branch from the ground, and with this he sliced out like it was a sabre, putting the Frenchman on the defensive, staggering him backward, inspiring me to hurriedly move in at him from behind.

Yet Holmes cried savagely:

"Step away, Watson, for I mean to take him!"

I obeyed this directive and retreated a number of paces from this contest, which reached its denouement with a startling suddenness as Holmes first stung the man's hand with the branch, knocking away the knife, and then with a fist he struck his opponent a furious blow to the temple, and a second to the chin as he teetered reeling about, sending him unconscious to the forest floor.

"Quickly, Sister!" he cried to our companion, who had been standing a distance away from the contest. "Inside the innermost pocket of my Ulster is some cord. Bring it so I might bind him."

As Sister Claire did so, Holmes, his breath heavy, stared down at the supine figure with a look of triumphant exaltation.

"I think you enjoyed that," I judged.

"There is much joy in defeating the wicked, Watson. Do you not feel it to be so?"

"Oh, yes," I said, "yes indeed."

Sister Claire hurried forward with the cords, and while Holmes and I held the dazed murderer to the earth, she skillfully secured his wrists, her knots cunning and tight.

"I learned to tie like this from my Uncle Pierre, who had been a sailor," she explained.

"Ha," chuckled Holmes, "then I do bless that man for the pragmatism of his tutelage."

"Are you harmed in any way, Sister?" I asked, peering at her neck, where the skin was unbroken by the blade, though a red mark lay on its surface.

"I am well, thank you Doctor Watson," she answered. "Though I think I shall bear bruises for a time. It is to God I give thanks that I felt him loosen his hold in the instant before he was to have slashed into me, and I reacted as you saw."

"With expertise, and the courage of a lioness!" Holmes judged, as impressed, as was I. "You saved not only yourself, but perhaps us as well, though we should of course have fought him most vigorously, even as we mourned your loss."

"Where did you learn to fight that way?" I inquired. "Again from your sailor uncle?"

She laughed in memory as she revealed:

"I had three older brothers, all rough and tumble, and from them I picked up little skills in hand to hand entanglements."

"This has all worked out like a miracle," I said.

"A miracle, yes," the nun agreed, "granted this day by God."

I could not help though to reflect on the death of the young man who had tried, at the last, to go right, and thought ahead once again to the pain which would be his mother's back at the convent.

A sound put an end to these thoughts, as I saw the criminal who would have slain the three of us as he had the ill-starred Jean-Claude, was stirring from the stupor of Holmes' blows, and after I had squatted down to draw him to a sitting pose, I asked him several simple questions to ascertain if were concussed, which I think he was not.

This done, Holmes pulled him, not too roughly, to his feet, and ordered:

"You will march with us back to the church, where the police will be summoned to take note of your many crimes. Watson, will you see to the cross, if you please?"

"No, let me convey it home," Sister Claire spoke up, and with doe-like grace she hurried over to where I had dropped the relic beside a mossy tree root. She lifted it almost as if it were a child, and cradled it in her arms, then I heard her pray:

"*Ah, sweet Queen of Heaven, never again let wicked men pry this from its sacred home.*"

*****

There was a surprise ahead, for mid-way to the church we saw coming toward us in the half-light of the gloaming now falling upon the world, the Mother Superior and two other nuns, as well as several men from the town, and out in front of all others, a trio of policeman, clad in uniforms of a blue that was both brighter yet paler than the bobbies wore back in London.

"I sent a young novice running to town to summon aid," Mother explained, as Holmes handed the now snarling criminal off to the authorities.

"I am glad you did," I told her.

"My little sister, have you been harmed?" Mother demanded of Sister Claire, reaching toward her neck with delicate fingers and tracing the red line the knife had left there, marking but not quite penetrating the skin.

I noted her first concern was for a person before her thoughts went to the cross Sister Claire still carried.

"I am well, Mother, I thank you," our companion in this deadly adventure replied in the simple language I had noticed nuns employed when speaking one to another.

"Then God be praised!" the Mother Superior declared. "And our cross! Our precious cross! Mr. Holmes, Doctor, and even you, Sister, you have succeeded in all ways today!"

In all ways that lay open to us, I thought, and wondered when one of us should reveal the fate of Sister Jeanne's son, who had been struck down so soon after taking up the straight and narrow path.

As it happened it would be the police who would make this revelation, for the oldest among them, a sergeant in residence in the nearby town, had spoken to each of we three in our stead, away from one another, and had listened with little expression to our accounts, which matched in every particular. After asking us to sign our statements, he thanked us, and let us be.

Before night was much older, the killer was transported to the town jail, there to await his trial, and as I would learn the next winter, his well-earned death below the blade of a guillotine. As for Holmes and I, we were invited back into the convent to witness, along with all the sisters save Jeanne, whom Mother allowed to take to her room to let loose her maternal grief, the return of the cross to its rightful place atop the altar.

"A far happier conclusion to this day than I would have thought possible at first light this morning," Mother proclaimed.

It was not proper, however, that men should remain within the convent, and after receiving the thanks of the order, the only fee Holmes would seek for solving the mystery, we were allowed to say a quick but heartfelt farewell out in the courtyard to Sister Claire, the young nun who had undertaken so much beside us that long day.

"Goodbye, my friends, and God bless you," she said, smiling but with tears, I think, barely contained within the brightness of her eyes. "I have never had such an adventure, and I shall not pass an hour but I will think of you both with great fondness."

"Nor I you," I told her, the sentiment heartfelt.

As for Holmes, he stared at her a moment, bowed deeply, and wordlessly took his leave.

*****

We walked back to the town under the light of a lovely

golden moon, nearly full, and knocked on the door of the inn there, to take a room until morning.

"Holmes," I asked, once we were about to turn in, each of our two beds smaller those in England, reminding me of those of children, "you were quite impressed with Sister Claire, were you not?"

"I was at that, Watson," he confessed as he lay down in the bed farthest from the door.

I saw a something akin to avuncular approval come into his eyes at mention of her, and he added:

"I will not be so arrogant as to say that such a mind as hers is wasted in a secluded life, as we all must choose our path, though in Paris she might have risen to great heights, and I will say the outer world's loss is the gain of any who might reside with her below the hallowed roof of her convent. Her story, I think, is far from finished, and may be grand indeed."

"Holmes," I noted, "you speak of our young companion in this case with what I might almost judge a certain vicarious pride."

"Do I, Watson?" he asked. "And why do you suppose that might be?"

"Well, I think you found in her a colleague, and almost a peer."

"A peer?" Holmes laughed now. "Hardly that, though had she been guided through the training that separates the true artist in the profession from a dogged bumbler such as Lestrade back home, and had she developed her skills of deduction to the fullest, there is much she might have been capable of."

"So it was a certain species of regret I saw in you as we parted from Sister Claire tonight? Regret for what will never be?"

"Perhaps," he allowed, "but I think there is something as yet ungrasped by you."

"Holmes?"

"As you know," he said, "my grandmother was French."

"Yes, though seldom do you confess that fact, I have noted," I said wryly.

"Nonsense, I take some pride in the heritage. Did you know, Watson, that my grandmother was Norman, and came from these parts?"

"I did not."

I realized he was confiding something profound, and my mind spun to pinpoint exactly what it was.

He laughed drowsily at my consternation and said:

"Even back in the hôtel lobby I recognized certain features in Sister Claire I once likewise saw in my grandmother, and think the young nun's demonstrated talents and mine may flow from a common ancestral spring."

"Are you saying Sister Claire may be some distant cousin?" I exclaimed.

"I think she is possibly," Holmes said at last, *family*."

BOOKS IN THE CONTINUING CHRONICLES OF SHERLOCK HOLMES

ABOUT THE AUTHOR

C. Thorne

C. Thorne is a writer who lives in the United States, and is a lifelong fan of Sir Arthur Conan Doyle's stories of the world's most famous fictional detective. He is the author of more than a thousand short stories, and nearly three-dozen books of prose and poetry, with even more tomes beneath his belt through the years as ghostwriter and contributor to a number of college-level textbooks. The Continuing Chronicles of  Sherlock Holmes is his most recent series, and a labor of love. He hopes you enjoy these stories as much as he and illustrator L. Thorne have enjoyed producing them.

CONTACT US

We love to hear from our fans. You are the reason we create. Without you, our dearest and most dedicated readers, we would not keep uncovering more, never-before-revealed Sherlock Holmes' adventures. Thank you for such positive feedback. It means so much to us! www.c-thorne-publishing@hotmail.com

LINK TO AMAZON

C. Thorne now presents many exciting, never-before revealed adventures of the greatest detective of all time, Mr. Sherlock Holmes. There are many more to come.
Please peruse them all!

Go to:
The Continuing Chronicles of Sherlock Holmes

Made in United States
Orlando, FL
29 June 2025